SCAPEGOAT
FOR A STUART

Recent Titles by Elizabeth Elgin from Severn House

ECHO OF A STUART

FOOTSTEPS OF A STUART

WHISPERS ON THE WIND

SCAPEGOAT FOR A STUART

Elizabeth Elgin

This edition first published in Great Britain 1999 by
SEVERN HOUSE PUBLISHERS LTD of
9–15 High Street, Sutton, Surrey SM1 1DF.
Originally published in 1975 in Great Britain by
Robert Hale Ltd. under the pseudonym *Kate Kirby*.
This title first published in the USA 1999 by
SEVERN HOUSE PUBLISHERS INC., of
595 Madison Avenue, New York, NY 10022.

British Library Cataloguing in Publication Data

Elgin,   Elizabeth
            Echo of a Stuart
            1.   Great Britain - History - James I, 1603-1625 - Fiction
            2.   Historical fiction
            1.   Title
            823.9'14 [F]

            ISBN 0-7278-5385-6

Printed and bound in Great Bri
MPG Books Ltd, Bodmin, Cor

CHAPTER ONE

1603

THE man with the faded red hair tipped the wine flagon yet again.

"Talk has it the Tudor bastard is dying."

He made the statement with no more feeling than a man might at the dying of a stray wolfhound bitch or that it should be an everyday occurrence for a Queen of England to lay close to death.

"Aye, sir, I've heard such talk . . ."

The young seaman raised his head. His eyes, heavy-lidded from too little sleep and too much wine, took on a reluctant expression as if it was beyond his understanding that one so exalted should suddenly become mortal. Elizabeth Tudor was a part of England. She couldn't die—could she?

He opened his mouth to protest, then thought better of it. Here in France the Queen of England was still dubbed bastard and Nan Bullen who bore her a witch and a whore.

"There is always talk," he shrugged. "It costs nothing. I only know the Queen was still alive a week gone when we sailed from Billingsgate, though God knows what might have happened by the time we get back . . ."

He lifted his shoulders in a gesture of resignation.

". . . if we *ever* get back!"

For three days the early spring gales had lashed the waters of the Channel into a fury and no shipping had left Gravelines and none entered. If the Goddamned weather didn't change soon, he fretted, he'd have drunk himself sober again in this stinking French tavern.

But no matter; the wine he tossed down his throat was costing nothing. If the old man was fool enough to pay for it, then let him.

He looked again at his drinking companion. It struck him as odd that the man's bearing and speech were those of a gentleman, though his appearance belied it. His clothes were homespun yet his boots were spurred and he carried a rapier.

"Are you a Londoner, sir?"

"No, boy, I was born in the north . . ." The guarded eyes did not waver; ". . . near York."

"Ah, York."

That city of churches where the people were a race apart. Oh, yes, he'd heard of York.

And soon, the seaman knew, this Northerner would ask the question so many of them asked.

'Can you tell me, lad, where I might clap eyes on Humphrey of the merchantman *Gillyflower*?'

Or he might say, 'I seek a kinsman of mine—a distant cousin who sails between the Port of London and Gravelines.'

They were usually his kinsmen or his friends, the seaman pondered. Always they sought a favour of him and often they had the bearing of noble birth and the clothes of a wanderer. Sometimes, too, they had the soft white hands of a priest.

But Humphrey cared little whether they were Romanist exiles or Jesuits from Douai. So long as their money rang true, be it in English gold or French, it was all the same to him.

Soon this man who urged wine upon him would ask the question and when the gale had blown itself out and the men and women who waited in the crowded inns at Nieuport and Dunkirk had gathered on the quayside at Gravelines, Humphrey would smuggle the man aboard the *Gillyflower* and hide him until the flat French coastline was lost from sight.

Then, with the Channel behind them and they had nosed safely up the Thames, it would doubtless be worth another gold angel to slip him over the rail into the wherry that would glide alongside from the darkness of the riverside. It would be easy then for a man who had no papers and gold in his pocket to slip into London unseen and vanish completely into the tangle of crowded streets.

The man refilled the glasses. He must get back to England for soon, surely, there would be another on Elizabeth Tudor's throne; a prince who would show favour to those who had been persecuted for their faith.

Mary Stuart, that prince's mother, had died for it and he who now sat hopefully in the tavern at Gravelines had lost his inheritance for it. James Stuart would be generous to those who had suffered in his mother's cause. Soon, thought the man, with the new King's blessing, he could journey home to Aldbridge and take back what was rightly his; those lands Elizabeth Tudor had taken from his father and given to another.

The man with the faded red hair edged closer.

"Tell me, lad," he whispered, "would you perchance know Humphrey who sails on the *Gillyflower*?"

*　　*　　*

James Stuart pulled his furs around him. God's blood, but it would be good to be in London. They said the English air was warmer and the sun shone stronger than it did in Scotland.

Outside all was grey, for winter had not yet loosened its hold on the north of Britain and the wind blew without mercy through every ill-fitting window and under every door of the palace of Holyrood.

The King of Scotland shivered. The winter had been unusually long. Already it was March and he had not yet been able to take his Spring bath.

He sighed and sniffed. The goosegrease could stay there a little longer; it wouldn't do to catch a chill when any day now there might be news from London.

Already Englishmen were travelling across the Marches, braving the wild border clans in their eagerness to curry favour with the king-elect. The man who came today— Thomas Percy of Northumberland's family—had been yet another of them.

"Esme, dear man, what did ye think to the Englishman?" the King enquired lazily of his companion. "Is it not fine that some already acknowledge me as Cousin Tudor's heir?"

"Aye, Majesty, it is. There's a good inheritance waiting in the south. But do ye no' think it might be wiser to tread warily for a while longer?"

James Stuart glared petulantly at his kinsman. It could only be a matter of time before England was his. Hadn't Robert Cecil promised it would be? Had not he, James Stuart, schemed and fawned and flattered these last twenty years to stay in Elizabeth Tudor's favour? And shouldn't England be his, anyway, by divine right of the Tudor blood that ran in his veins?

"What ails ye, Esme? Soon I'll be running my hands through England's gold, so mind your clack!"

"Sire, I meant no harm. I only felt that if ye make promises to the Papists, it might not set well wi' the men at Westminster. They've got Protestant leanings, the men who advise Elizabeth Tudor."

"Aye, and Thomas Percy promised me the support of the English Papists if I'd let them hear their mass in peace, so I'll wed the one and woo the other until I'm proclaimed in London. I care nothing for Protestants or Papists. I want England, Esme! I'm a Stuart and my grand-dam was Henry

8

Tudor's sister. I've a right to England, as my mother had."

"Aye, but I did no' see ye tearing over the border, screaming for revenge when your cousin Elizabeth cut off the poor creature's head!"

"How could I? My mother was a Papist. Would ye have had me ruin my chances in England? And anyway, the woman plotted treason against Cousin Tudor. Do ye not know her foolishness could have lost me the succession?"

James Stuart was becoming angry. My, he thought, but he'd be glad when the English matter had been settled. One false move even now and Arabella Stuart and her grasping old grand-dam at Hardwick could get the lot!

"Ye're a hard man, Jamie Stuart, so ye are! Did ye feel nothing when the poor woman lost her head? Your own mother?"

"*My own mother?* A woman I'd never clapped eyes on? And ye're right, I can be hard when I fix my mind on it, so nae forget it!"

"Then go easy, Sire. Elizabeth Tudor hasn't named her successor, yet. Make no promises that would anger the English."

"Promises, Esme, were aye made to be broken."

The pale watery eyes narrowed into shifty slits.

"I only told Master Percy that if I became King of England I would likely allow each man to worship according to his conscience—if he behaved himself."

"Aye and he'll be away to England and blether it all over the place that the Scottish king will bring his Mam's religion wi' him when he rides over the border! It'll do ye no good!"

"Esme. Esme, dear man—"

Affectionately James stroked his companion's hand.

"I need all the friends I can gather until I'm sure of the English throne; I want a safe passage to Westminster, that's all!"

He stroked his small square beard and his eyes scanned the distant hills as if he was trying to see beyond them to the Utopia that lay only a grasp away to the south.

"Only let them proclaim me King of England and I'll have no need o' the Papists; *no need at all*!"

*   *   *

There was a stillness over London; a strange brooding that hushed the streets and stilled the tongues of church bells.

For three days the Queen had lain sick. Across the fields at the palace of Richmond, death had sidled close to Elizabeth Tudor.

"She will not take her physic," Lady Scrope whispered tearfully. "She sits on the floor refusing to eat or speak. Nor will she take to her bed for fear she will not rise from it again."

"Has Her Grace spoken yet?"

The small hunchbacked man was anxious.

"Has she named her successor?"

"Only to say that her throne is the throne of Kings."

"And the Scotsman . . . ?"

Lady Scrope shook her head.

"She mentioned no one. 'He that is base-born shall not have my realm' is all she has said."

Robert Cecil raised his eyes to the ceiling of the ante-room.

"Lord, was there ever such a woman?"

"No, Master Secretary, there never was nor ever will be again!"

With trembling lips, the Queen's cousin picked up a silver bowl and set it on a salver.

"And now, with your leave sir, I must go to my lady."

But the wizened old woman waved aside the broth.

"Take it away," she croaked.

Could they not understand that every sip she took was an

agony of knife thrusts? Surely the abscess in her throat must burst soon?

"Philadelphia, my bones hurt. Place another cushion at my back."

"Your Grace, the floor is no fit place for the Queen of England. Will you not rest on your bed?"

Wearily Elizabeth Tudor shook her head. She wanted to scream at them all to leave her in peace. She wanted to pace the floor and rage at those who hovered around her, waiting for her to hand her kingdom to James Stuart.

Well, let them wait. England's throne was still hers and she would give it away with her last breath and not one gasp before!

Lord, how her throat hurt. She was dying, she knew it. Every bone in her body ached for its death-sleep.

It is awful, she thought, to be so alone; to die amidst a crowd, yet be so lonely.

Where were they, those people she had loved? Where were Kat Ashley and Burghley, Robin Dudley and Kate Carey? They had been with her for so long and now they were dead, memories like the sunlit days of her youth.

Once she had flamed fierce and eager and Robin had galloped to Hatfield and laid his heart at her feet; Robin, love of her life.

On that day at Hatfield they brought Mary's ring to her, the black and gold token that once betrothed her half-sister to the King of Spain. She had known then that England was hers.

Now they waited for *her* ring. They filed it from her swollen finger before Christmas and she had been filled with horror and desolation at the very nature of the act. But it was still with her. She closed her fingers around it and felt its severed edges sharp against the palm of her hand. And when she was dead they would run with it to the man she knew was waiting outside and he would speed it away into the night, to Scotland.

"Lord, let me not die in the darkness," she prayed.

Then she stirred angrily on her cushions. She wasn't dead yet! The ring was safe in her keeping and she was still the Queen of England! Perversely she stuck her thumb into her mouth and sucked it as she had done so long ago in her frightened childhood.

In the courtyard, booted and spurred with his horse saddled at the ready, Sir Robert Carey waited on standby to ride to Edinburgh.

"Mother of God," he fretted, "will they never bring the ring?"

* * *

In the elm-wood rocking-cot by Beth Weaver's bed, a newly-born baby nuzzled the pillow, her pink and perfect mouth searching instinctively for the comfort of a warm breast.

Outside, beneath a sky changed suddenly from the grey of winter to a pale and gentle blue, a song-thrush promised that spring was close at hand.

Beth Weaver was happy, even though she knew that her little daughter would almost certainly be the last of her children. When a woman nears thirty-three, she must accept that her child-bearing years are well-nigh over.

The woman who sat by the bedside knitted slowly, her gnarled hands clumsy with age. With a downward thrust of her foot, she set the cot swaying gently.

"Have you decided on a name for the babe, yet? Tomorrow she must be carried to the church. She will be nearly two days old by then and a christening cannot be so long delayed, daughter."

Beth reached for the old hands, gently stilling the irregular clicking of the needles.

"I have decided what my new daughter shall *not* be called, my lady."

She lay back on her pillows, smiling contentment.

"Have you thought, madam, that each of my babes has been called for the dead? Diccon was called for Jeffrey's son whom the Spaniards killed and Margaret was christened for Meg, your daughter. Then Jane was called for my mother, God rest her, and Peter for the father I never knew."

"You are right; I had not realised it." Anne Weaver nodded. "What name have you in mind for the little one?"

"Yours, my lady; I shall name her for you."

"Nay, Beth."

Despite the pleasure in her voice, the old woman shook her head.

"If the babe is to be called for the living, why take the name of one who is near-dead? I am old, in my seventieth year."

"Still, for the love I bear you, I would give the baby your name, my lady mother. Harry will agree with me when he returns, I know it."

"Ha! That son of mine is never at hand when he is needed."

Deftly Anne Weaver changed the subject.

"Skipping off to York at yester-sunrise and his wife the lighter of a fat little daughter at sundown!"

She stilled her foot on the rocking-cot and eased her body into a more comfortable position.

"But do you not think, Beth, that it would be unwise to have two of the same name in one house? Wouldn't it make for confusion?"

"Surely not, madam, for you are the Lady Anne and the babe would be *little* Anne."

"Then call her little Anne. Call her Anna. It's a gentle-sounding name and one that would please me."

"Anna Weaver," Beth repeated the name.

She sighed happily. She was, she knew, the most cosseted, the best-loved wife in the whole of York's vast county. Even yet, after sixteen years of marriage, the sight and touch of her husband could send the colour flaming to her cheeks and the small pulse at her throat beating giddily. To be so loved was to walk constantly through a soft, warm cloud. It seemed impossible now to think of life without Harry, yet once she had refused him in marriage.

That day, from all her yesterdays, stood out clear and frightening. That day she could have thrown away a world of happiness had not the boy she loved returned from the wars a lusting man, sweeping her protests and refusals aside.

Harry had not cared when she told him she was a plough-man's bastard or that the man her mother had married had been cuckolded; that even as they repeated their reluctant marriage vows, the woman at his side already carried another's child.

Where was he now, that man who walked out of their home never to return? Had he died without knowing the daughter he thought was his was now a mother, five times over?

Deep within her, Beth had been glad to learn she was not that strange man's daughter. Better by far to have been fathered in love by a ploughman than in respectable hatred by a man her mother had cause to loathe, even before he placed the marriage ring on her finger.

Gently Beth placed the old hand to her cheek.

"My lady," she whispered, "you have been so good to me . . ."

Anne Weaver smiled gently. It had not been hard to love her son's wife.

14

"Beth, love, I wanted you for my daughter from the moment I laid eyes on you. I loved you and at the same time I could have shaken you senseless for refusing to marry Harry!"

"Your son was noble-born, my lady, and I had just learned I was a bastard."

"You were the maid my son wanted and you were my Meg come back to me from the dead."

Anne Weaver sighed, thinking back to that day when Harry returned home after the Armada fighting.

She had laughed and cried and declared there should be a great celebration. But Harry had whispered tersely that there could be no feasting, for Diccon was dead. Diccon, Jeffrey's first-born, had died in Harry's arms.

Then, with his jaws clamped tight in a face white with grief, Harry had ridden furiously to York and the girl he swore he would wed.

Dearest Beth, who had brought Meg back from her lonely grave; Beth who stood uncertain at Harry's side with hair the colour of palest gold and blue, bewildered eyes that were unfathomably sad. Meg's hair; Meg's eyes.

For a moment in time the world rocked beneath Anne's feet and she had reached out with eager arms to Meg's reincarnation.

In that moment of blinding joy, Anne would have wanted Beth if the devil himself had spawned her.

Stiffly she rose to her feet.

"The babe is sleeping and so must you, sweet Beth. I will send Agnes to you with a posset."

The old woman leaned over the cot.

"Sleep you well, baby Anna."

She turned slowly at the doorway, nodding her head.

"I like the name; yes, I like it well. Today, when Harry

15

and John return, we will carry our dearest Anna to her christening."

*   *   *

Spring came early to Escorial. The Spanish sun kissed warm the courtyard stones and gentled the almond trees into full blossoming. The sky was wide and blue, but the man who sat chin on hand by the fountain felt no uplifting of his heart.

"Idiot that the man is," he fretted.

Philip of Spain was a fool, a weak, miserly fool! Elizabeth Tudor was dying. Any day now her throne could pass to Scotland's King and with a little pressure from Spain and Rome, James Stuart might well be guided into the ways of the old religion again. Mary Stuart's son should, at the very least, allow freedom of worship to England's persecuted Romanists.

Only *now* was the time for action whilst James Stuart was still unsure of what awaited him in England and before the foxy little Cecil could exert his influence over the weak-willed Scot. Next year, next month even might be too late, yet the Spanish king was pleading poverty and refusing to give any help or offer any comfort.

"I am wasting my time here!"

The man jerked to his feet and kicked petulantly at a stone.

He was not aware that the man who watched from the shadows had quietly approached and now walked at his side.

"Sir, that poor pebble must have offended you greatly," the stranger remarked amiably, smiling into the brooding blue eyes.

"You do not remember me? Have you forgotten your schooldays in the Horse Fair, Master Fawkes?"

The face that pictured black misery broke into a smile of mingled pleasure and disbelief.

"Kit! It is Christopher Wright!"

He held out his hands in greeting.

"By Our Lady, old friend, it is good to see you. It is good to hear a York voice in all this Spanish babble!"

He laughed loudly, the cloud that wrapped him round forgotten.

"I can't believe it, Christopher. What are you doing here?"

There was a moment of hesitation, an almost intangible pause, then,

"I must beg the question, Guy, and ask the same of you."

Englishmen who met at the Spanish Court must be sure of their friends before they answered questions.

"I am here, Christopher, on a matter of business and I have not done well. King Philip is not in a helpful mood."

"Then you have a kindred spirit for I too did not find what I came to seek."

"You came from England?"

"Aye—and you?"

"I travelled here from the Netherlands."

Again there was an uncertain silence, then,

"Tell me, Christopher, how is England? I have not seen it these many years."

"Elizabeth Tudor is dying—she may even now be dead and it is said that Robert Cecil has been having a fruitful correspondence with James of Scotland. Master Cecil fancies himself as a kingmaker!"

"I feared it." Fawkes shook his head. "I feared all along we would be too late . . ."

He stopped abruptly; he had said too much. Then he raised his eyes and read understanding in those of his companion.

"Damnation!" he swore softly. "This is no time for faint

17

hearts! I will tell you my business, Christopher. I was sent here to plead help for those in England who suffer for their faith."

He felt again the warm handclasp.

"And I am here on a like errand. I am sent by—by a certain London gentleman."

"Then it is true that there are many in England who still profess the old faith? I feared the Queen and her priest-hunters had almost done for it."

"No, Guy. Priests travel from Douai to spread the gospel and bring the succour of the Mass. They go in fear of their lives but there are many Englishmen who give them food and shelter."

"It is good to hear it," Fawkes smiled warmly. "There may be hope for us, yet. When the Queen is dead, it may well be that King James will allow men to worship as they please."

Christopher Wright creased his forehead into a frown.

"You say *hope for us*, yet I have it in my mind from our schooldays, Guy, that you were not of the faith of Rome."

"Nor was I. I was reared in my father's religion, God spare his miserable Protestant soul, but my widowed mother had the good sense to re-marry—a Master Bainbridge. He is a Romanist, and they live near Knaresborough. It is Romanist country in those parts—there are many of the Percy clan living close at hand."

He shrugged his shoulders.

"It became natural to shelter priests and listen to their teachings. I embraced the true faith and received the Sacrament a little before my coming of age."

"And then you took up soldiering?"

"Aye, I fought for Spain. What else could I do? My mother and my step-father had gone through my inheritance before I had the chance to lay hands on it."

He grinned cheerfully. The spendthrift living of his mother's

18

second husband was more acceptable than his father's frugal ways had been. Fawkes was fond of old Dionysius Bainbridge.

"Are the Spaniards good masters?"

"They are—I learned much from them. Without boasting, Kit, there can be few men in England who have my skill with gunpowder. I can lay and fire a trail and use a slow-match with the best of men. But I fear there will be little use for the skills of a professional soldier in England."

"You intend to go home, then?"

"Yes, I must. I have the urge to see my mother before she dies and to hear my native tongue again; I want to hear the bells of York as I did in my boyhood."

"And are they the only reasons for your return, Guy?"

The two men eyed each other, some of their earlier caution returning.

"No, friend, they are not. I'll tell you in truth that I think when the King of Scotland inherits England, he will show mercy to those who now must worship in secret; for his mother's sake, I feel it will be so. It would be good to be able to pray again without fear, in England."

"And if he does not show mercy? If James Stuart takes up where Elizabeth Tudor left off—what then?"

A faraway look came into the soldier's eyes and it seemed that he was searching his heart for a great truth.

"Then I shall have had all the more reason for returning home, for our people may be in need of a faith such as mine!"

CHAPTER TWO

THE Minster clock chimed out noon-day as Harry Weaver and his father, Sir John, rode beneath the massive bulk of Micklegate Bar and turned their horses' heads to the north-west, picking up the old Roman road that ran straight and true as a speeding arrow from York to Aldbridge.

Only that morning a Queen's Messenger had ridden in from the south, carrying news of Elizabeth Tudor's death and bearing instructions that the Lord Mayor proclaim James Stuart as King of England. And he had done it from each Bar in the city walls and released such a wave of rejoicing that it seemed the great Elizabeth was already forgotten.

John Weaver's shoulders drooped dejectedly. There could never again be a monarch quite like Elizabeth Tudor, he thought. She had held his heart captive in her exquisite hands from the moment he raised his eyes to hers. She had glittered and gleamed like a million jewels and paled the sun that shone through the great window behind her. In John Weaver's heart, Elizabeth of England was young and vibrant still and not a wizened, half-forgotten old woman whose tired face had even now been moulded into its death-mask.

Perhaps, he reasoned, to keep Elizabeth young had been to keep himself young and Anne, too. Whilst Elizabeth Tudor had lived, neither he nor Anne could be old.

But now in the streets of York, folk talked as though it were a job well done that the Queen had gone at last.

"Old, by Our Lady! Nigh on seventy!"

"Thought she'd hang on for ever!"

"Nice to have a King again."

"Two princes and a princess for the succession!"

Suddenly John too felt old. Behind him, within York's defending walls, there would already have begun a hustle of preparation, of sweetening of houses and swilling of streets. There would be a turmoil of speech-writing, a turning-out of closets and an airing of finery as the city made ready to receive its new King.

And the inn-keepers and tavern-owners would be licking their lips at thoughts of the gold that would find its way into their pockets from the insurge of half the county.

"When will he come?"

"What is he like?"

"Is it true he'll grant freedom of worship to all men, even to Romanists?"

"Long live good King James!"

They were already turning their eyes northward as if they expected to see him in that instant, riding triumphantly to receive the homage of the second city in his realm before progressing south, to London.

Well, let them welcome Mary Stuart's son before the Queen's old bones had time to set in the shape of death; there was one Yorkshireman who would mourn her and weep in his heart at her passing.

"God grant Your Grace rest," John whispered, "and receive your sweet soul."

*   *   *

Lady Anne Weaver creased her forehead into a frown as the death bell began to toll.

Testily, she picked up her cane and hobbled to the door of the winter-parlour, agitated by the awesome sound of the low-pitched ringing.

21

"Agnes? Come here will you, woman?" she called, silently cursing her own slowness and Agnes Muff's deafness, trying to close her ears to the sound that reminded her with God-like resonance of her own precarious state of mortality.

The fat old cook was standing at the kitchen window, her hand cupped around her ear.

"Be that t'death-bell, then?"

"Aye, Agnes, it is, but who could have died is a mystery to me."

"There's none ailing in the village as far as I know, my lady, and no prayers asked last Sunday, either."

"Then it's a mystery Sir John might well be able to unravel," Anne whispered as the scraping of horses' hooves over the stableyard cobbles filled her heart with a mingling of relief and pleasure. John and Harry were back from York and all was well again.

But the sight of her husband's taut face caused Anne's heart to skip a beat.

"What is it, John? Who has died? Who does the bell ring for?"

John reached out for his wife's hand.

"Come inside, my lady, for what I have to tell you will not make pretty hearing."

He waited until they were alone, then gently taking her hands in his, he said,

"She is dead, love. Our Queen is dead."

"Elizabeth Tudor dead?" she whispered, her voice like that of a far-away stranger.

She shivered as death's angel reached out and brushed her face with an icy wing. In crooking a finger at England's Queen, he was whispering a warning to her, for as long as the Queen had lived, so she too, Anne had thought, could defy time.

Now she felt tired and afraid.

"God rest her soul," Anne whispered, crossing herself as she still sometimes did. "Who tolls the bell for her?"

"It is old Barnabas," John replied. "I asked him if he could pull on the rope until sundown and he said he'd keep the bell ringing until Doomsday, if needs be."

Would that Barnabas could live long enough to toll the death-bell for him, thought John, for there was no-one who could pull as long and strong as the old fox-catcher. Barnabas knew well how Lucifer and his demons feared the sound of the ringing of a bell; knew too that when a soul left the keeping of its earthly body, there was a fearful commotion let loose with devils and angels fighting to possess it.

What more natural then, than to ring the sombre old bell at a soul's passing; to toll it loud and long on the side of the angels?

And not until darkness sent those demons back to the devil their master, would Barnabas cease his fervent ringing.

Suddenly John felt the burden of every day of his seventy-two years. Elizabeth Tudor was dead and with her she had taken his youth and almost all memory of it.

Could he, John wished, but strike a bargain with the Almighty, he would willingly surrender the remainder of his years in exchange for one short hour of his youth. And granted that hour, he would take it from the precious day so long ago when Walter Skelton, the journeyman-weaver, arrived with his little donkey at the door of John's farmstead; the day, unknown to John, that Mary Stuart had been secreted into captivity in Castle Bolton on nearby Redmire Moor. That fateful day had seen the spawning of an intrigue that was to set John's world awry and become the cause of Meg's cruel death.

But they had not known those things on the soft July evening of Walter's arrival. Anne's face had flushed with pleasure at the sight of their old friend and Meg had run laughing to greet him, the pale, soft hair that floated about her touched with the red of the tired sun.

They lived at the farm overlooking the green, then. John had worked the land in the summer months and plied his own trade in the cold of winter, shuttling and treading out fine woollen cloth. They had prospered; Anne sung at her work and Meg had dreamed by the hearth of Kit Wakeman.

The lord of the manor of Aldbridge was Sir Crispen Wakeman, not a man called John who once served his time as a weaver and Meg had been troth-plighted to Jeffrey.

But they had not married, for Meg had borne a love-child instead, then died with her lover's name on her lips.

Harry, the child who was all that was left to them now of their daughter, whom men knew as Sir John Weaver's son.

John wrenched his thoughts back from the sweet ache of times remembered.

"They proclaimed the Stuart in York. Talk has it that he'll journey to London by way of the city. There's a great to-do there amongst the Guilds and the City Fathers."

"Pah!" Anne spat. "Did Elizabeth name him, then?"

"Aye, love, it was her dying wish that James Stuart should succeed her."

"By Our Lady," Anne whispered, "I never thought I'd live long enough to see a Stuart on England's throne."

"We must accept the Queen's right to dispose of her kingdom as she thought best," John reasoned.

"Oh, I'll grant you that, husband, but it's my opinion that none of *her* ilk should have claim to anything that is English," Anne retorted, bitterly.

John was silent for a moment. Even after so many years, he thought, Anne found it difficult to say that name.

Her ilk, she said; Mary Stuart's kin, she meant.

So long gone, yet festering still in Anne's heart was the knowledge that those who had plotted for Mary Stuart had been the cause of Meg's death. Meg had learned of the plot to seize Elizabeth Tudor's throne for Scottish Mary and Kit Wakeman, one of those plotters, had falsely accused Meg of witchcraft to ensure her silence.

John was a fair-minded man.

"James of Scotland has Tudor blood," he said. "He has claim to England through Margaret Tudor, King Henry's sister."

Anne set John's boots side by side in the wide stone hearth.

"I don't want to talk of the Stuarts," she muttered, "and you'd better arrange for prayers for the Queen."

Then she raised her hands in mock-horror.

"Jesu, and I should forget the great news!" she gasped. "Where is Harry? Oh, it's true, when God takes, he also gives in return!"

She laughed with delight, glad to be able to replace the news of the Stuart succession with something more to her liking.

"Our dearest Beth is the lighter of a bonny little maid," she said triumphantly. "Now there's something worth the telling, eh, husband?"

There was a clattering of booted feet on the polished holly-wood of the staircase outside.

"And there goes Harry to see his wife and little daughter. I'll warrant Agnes Muff gave him the news as he came in from the stables."

John smiled tenderly.

"Does Beth do well, and the babe?"

"Aye, thanks be. Come now, and I shall show you the babe."

Harry Weaver was lolling on his wife's bed, his arm around her shoulders, his face close to hers, when Anne and John entered the bedchamber.

"How now, my lady mother? Is not my little Anna most

fair? Is she not the spitting image of her father?" he laughed.

"Arrogant puppy!" Anne scolded fondly. "And take your great boots off the bed-cover, for I'll wager there's half the muck of the streets of York on them!"

"Arrogant, am I?" teased Harry, his handsome face alight with mischief, "then, my lady, it is all of your doing for I am your son!"

Abruptly Anne turned to the cot, unwilling to meet Harry's eyes for even yet, half a lifetime later, she could feel unease when reminded of Harry's parentage.

Aye lad, she thought, *arrogant you are and stubborn too when the mood is on you, but it's none of my doing, for the one you call father had no hand in your getting, nor are you of my body.*

She closed her eyes against the pain of remembering.

And your arrogance is of your noble breeding, for you got it from the one who sired you.

She said abruptly,

"We had planned, Beth and me, to have Anna carried to the church for her naming, but it must wait, now, until tomorrow. The church will be dressed for sorrow, I fear."

"My lady, I am right sorry to have brought such bad news home with me," Harry Weaver replied, "but the Queen was old. Maybe a new young King will be more to England's liking. There are some who have been praying for this acces-these many years.

"Oh? And who might they be? There have been no prayers in Aldbridge for James Stuart, that I tell you."

"No, my lady," Harry smiled at the old woman's indignance, "but then, there is no urge in Aldbridge for a Romanist prince."

"A *Romanist*, boy?"

"Aye, mother. For one whose accession might mean the granting of freedom of worship."

"There'll be no Popish prayers said in this manor!" Anne Weaver spat. "And besides, James Stuart was not reared a Papist."

"His mother was of the old faith, though. Mary Stuart died with latin prayers on her lips!"

"Aye, and she died for plotting against the lawful Queen of England, and never forget, Harry Weaver!"

Bright red patches flamed on Anne's cheeks.

John held up his hand, a look of warning silencing the younger man's indiscretion.

"Aye, and her son is not of the faith of Rome or he'd not have been given Elizabeth Tudor's blessing."

"Then why," Anne spluttered, "does this foolish jackanapes here talk of Romanist princes?"

"He doesn't love, he doesn't. What Harry meant was that those who cling to the old faith hope that James Stuart will show them leniency and let them pray according to their beliefs. Perhaps he will let them hear their Mass in the quiet of their own homes."

"With a priest of their own choosing? With a Jesuit from Douai to chant perdition and preach treason with every paternoster? God's blood, husband, have you forgotten what happened to our own little maid because of Mary Stuart and her Popish prayers? Meg was of my body and grew to beauty at my breast. I will never forget why she died. Whilst I draw breath I shall curse all Stuarts with the blooming of every heartsease. I shall curse them with my last breath and think it well-spent!"

"But my lady," Harry Weaver interposed, "surely you know that King James's wife is of the Roman faith?"

"I know no such thing, young master. Folks said she took instruction from a French priest after she wed James Stuart, but I'll warrant there'll be no Popish chantings allowed when

27

she comes to the English Court. Robert Cecil will see to it that Danish Anna . . ."

Anne stopped abruptly, closing her eyes against the shock of realisation, feeling the blood drain from her face.

"My lady?" Beth Weaver called from her bed. "What is the matter? Go to her, husband," she urged, "and beg her pardon for upsetting her so foolishly."

Beth held out her arms to the old woman who stood trembling by the window.

"Dear lady, I beg of you not to fret. My Harry was thoughtless in what he said. He meant no harm. Only tell me what riles you and we shall have it set to rights."

Anne Weaver took a deep breath, fighting to control the furious thumping of her heart.

"Nay, Beth, I fear it is too late to set to rights what we have done between us this day, for even now Father Good-body will have writ it in readiness in the Parish Book."

"Madam?"

"Can't you see what we have done, daughter? *We will call her Anna*, we said, and may God forgive us our stupidity for we have named this child for one of Mary Stuart's ilk. May the sweet babe never have cause to regret it, for I'd liefer have called her after the devil!"

Then suddenly as her fury had arisen, so it died and Anne Weaver hobbled painfully to the bedside cot.

"Sweetest little babe," she whispered, "I ask your forgiveness with all my heart, for were your grand-dam not so old and foolish, she'd have given you any name save that of a Stuart; any name at all!"

*   *   *

Charles James Stuart inhaled England's sweet April air and thrilled anew to the heady feeling of bewildered delight. The English succession had plagued him for more years than he cared to admit. Elizabeth Tudor's perversity had caused him sometimes to hope, sometimes to despair, and but for the clandestine guidance of Robert Cecil, he swore he'd have given up long ago.

Now he could scarcely believe the ease with which the accession was taking place and he smiled graciously to Sir Thomas Lake who rode beside him.

Of course, thought King James, Lake's presence at his side did not fool him at all, nor, for that matter, did that of the Dean of Canterbury. They had each, he knew, been sent by their respective masters; by Robert Cecil and Archbishop Whitgift to observe and to report, of that there was little doubt. But from his state of blissful contentment, James Stuart was willing to admit that no doubt those worthy gentlemen had good cause for their actions. After all, Cecil had worked hard and long to ensure that England's throne did not fall to a Romanist and the good Archbishop must have felt some apprehension about the new King's attitude to the English Church, or even have harboured misgivings about the wife of his new liege-lord. But Anna would drop her half-hearted Romanism like a hot tattie in return for the rewards that awaited her as the King of all Britain's consort.

James hoped his wife was behaving herself and not throwing another tantrum at being left at home in Scotland. But Anna was big with another child and could not be expected to make the journey. He'd been glad of the excuse to leave her behind. He wanted all the glory of the journey to London for himself and besides, he disliked having women around him, pregnant women especially.

Now Berwick and Newcastle, Durham and Richmond, were behind the King's cavalcade. Along almost every mile of their slow progress, men had gathered to see their new King pass. At every great house along the way, James had been fêted and fawned upon and his gentlemen-in-waiting forced to

29

commandeer carts and wagons as they journeyed south in order that the abundance of gifts the King was eagerly collecting might be conveyed in safety. James was beginning to enjoy himself now that the wild, endless moors on the one hand and the secret hidden valleys on the other had been safely traversed without sight or sound of a single witch.

Now before him lay the Plain of York, thick with forest, mile upon mile of it and signs of a prosperity and contentment he had never seen in his own country.

"How long to York, good Dean?"

"Scarce fifteen miles, Sire. It is a fine city and second only to London."

James leaned towards Sir Thomas, dropping his voice to a whisper.

"And will it be loyal, do you think? Does it still cleave to Rome in its secret heart?"

"No, Majesty. The Northerners learned their lesson long ago when they rose for . . ."

He stopped, wishing he could bite off his tongue before King James had it cut from his head. He had almost added, ". . . for the Scottish Queen."

But the Scottish Queen had been King James's mother and even if she had lost her head for conspiring against England's lawful ruler, there was no need now to remind her son of it.

"The Northerners are loyal, your Majesty. There are dissenters in their midst, but their numbers are small, Sire. There is no cause to fear them."

He glanced obliquely at his King, noting the way the royal fingers delicately caressed the squat royal beard, seeing anew the staring, bulbous eyes, the curled-up moustache, the flesh that was soft and moist as that of a woman.

True, Lake conceded, James Stuart sat a horse well. Astride a good beast, he looked for the most part a kingly figure.

Could he truly be so weak-legged or did his disability provide him with the excuse to need a shoulder to lean on—the shoulder, most often, of a pink-cheeked page-boy? But despite what might have been whispered to the contrary at his birth, James was Darnley's son and what was bred in the bone . . .

Sir Thomas shrugged away his thoughts, alarmed by their treasonable nature.

There was contentment on the face of the Dean of Westminster. The Very Reverend gentleman was well pleased with what he had so far seen of the new Defender of the Faith. James Stuart had been weaned onto the Holy Book. He could hold long and learned discussions with men of the Cloth and quote vast biblical passages with ease. It was becoming increasingly obvious that despite his rigid Protestant upbringing, James Stuart would embrace the Anglican mode of worship with the greatest of ease.

From the forefront of the procession, a troupe of riders detached themselves and rode off with a great clatter, split with meticulous fairness into equal parts of Scots and English; there would be none given cause to accuse James Stuart of favouritism.

Scotland and England now made up one powerful kingdom and wee Robbie Cecil could undertake the complicated task of uniting their laws and customs, decided the King of All Britain. For the moment it was sufficient that outriders were speeding ahead to warn the Lord Mayor and Aldermen of York that James Stuart was approaching. He had expressed a wish that his ministers should journey from London and meet him at York, bringing with them coaches fit for a King of England to ride in and jewels, regalia and heralds. Now he wanted them brought to him so that he might enter his second city proudly and not as the poverty-stricken ruler he had once been.

The King straightened his back and lifted his chin. Life was suddenly almost unbelievably good. It was nearly a month now since Carey had dropped Elizabeth Tudor's severed ring into his hand and so far, he had been well received in England. He had been showered with speeches of welcome and costly gifts to prove the flowery addresses. He was becoming rich beyond his wildest fancies and there was more, much much more to come!

My, he thought, running the tip of his tongue round his thick, wet lips, life was good now for Jamie Stuart.

CHAPTER THREE

THE pot-man with the faded red hair set down tankards and a jug of ale, then quietly withdrew to his seat behind the settle.

The *Irish Boy* was a quiet inn where for the most part men seemed to toss down their drink quickly and talk quietly and earnestly. And sometimes there were those with the restless eyes who sat alone in the gloom of a quiet corner. They weren't so hard to recognise, those spies of Cecil's. Indeed, they were so thick on the ground these days that it was small wonder their master knew what was in a man's mind almost before a man knew it himself.

But today there were none of Cecil's men in the *Irish Boy* and the two men the pot-man had just served were the more relaxed because of it.

"So you are leaving the plague behind you, eh, Tom, or are you away north to see the Queen?" the younger of the two men quipped with mock solemnity.

"I am travelling to Alnwick on business for my cousin the Earl, good Robert. As for the plague," he shrugged, "soon there'll be no place free of it if many more Londoners insist on travelling north to meet Queen Anna. But I care nothing for her. The Stuart's woman is a feckless creature; a broodmare for the provision of heirs."

"Hold up there, Master Percy! Any more such talk and our new King will be relieving you of your position at Court. I thought you were happy with the Scotsman's crowning?"

Thomas Percy's ruddy complexion flushed redder still.

"I don't know what to think. I hoped James Stuart would show mercy to those of the old faith, but now I am not so sure. He seems to think of little else but following the hunt!"

The man from Beverley glared into his ale.

"I tell you, Robert, it is Cecil who rules this land and so long as James Stuart can hunt and play kiss-in-the-ring with pretty page boys, he's happy to let him!"

"And . . . ?"

"Well, can't you see the way of it? James Stuart trusts Cecil and Cecil hates Romanism, so what price now the Stuart's promises to allow us freedom of worship?"

The younger of the two men stared gloomily into his empty tankard.

"Cecil's spies are everywhere. They are in every foreign Court and they miss nothing. If the King of Spain changed his hose, Cecil would know about it."

"Then he'll know that Christopher Wright visited the Spanish Court and met the powderman there?"

"Aye, though he'll not know who sent him, so *I'll* not worry over that. But I think we should give things a try, Tom. It might well be that James Stuart will try to keep his word, in spite of Cecil. And if he doesn't—well, there will be ways . . ."

"And the sooner the better, for I'm sick of waiting. You mentioned a powderman. Oh, but that gives me ideas, Robert! It makes me wish I knew how to handle gunpowder."

"God's death, Tom, you are a fool!" hissed his companion. "We all get ideas, but we do not give them voice in a London tavern. Even in this place, we cannot be sure. We must go easily, I tell you. Take yon' pot-man."

He inclined his head towards the settle.

"Who is he? Where is he from?"

"It's all right, he's one of us. He wouldn't work here if he wasn't."

"Even so, I'm not sure of him. He's too meek, too quiet. He misses nothing, I'll be bound."

"I tell you he's all right. I'll swear, Robert, you see Cecil's men at every verse-end!"

He swung round defiantly in his seat.

"Here, man!" He snapped his fingers. "More ale, an' it please you!"

The elderly man rose to his feet, his face a mask of indifference.

"Is there more I can do, sirs?"

His servile manner made a mockery of the proud tilt of his head and the arrogance in his eyes.

"You can fill our tankards and take a sup for yourself. Have it here, with us."

"As you please, sir."

He raised his tankard.

"To your good health, masters."

The man who had ordered the ale nodded in acknowledgement, his eyes narrowed into slits.

"You are new to this inn, friend. Where did you come from?"

"From Yorkshire—originally."

"And before that?"

"Does it matter?" the pot-man shrugged. "The landlord is satisfied with my work. If there is anything in my manner that displeases you . . . ?"

The men's eyes met, those of the inquisitor acknowledging silently that perhaps after all there was something unusual about the red-haired man.

"There is nothing that displeases us," the younger man interposed gently, "but you are new to this tavern and my friend is curious."

Gently his foot nudged Percy's under cover of the table in a leave-it-to-me gesture.

35

"You are from Yorkshire, you say? My friend here rides to Yorkshire tonight and thence to Northumberland."

"Then I envy him. It is a long time since I set foot on my own soil."

"How long, Master Pot-man?"

"More than fifteen years."

"So you are a man of York?" Tom Percy took up the questioning again. "And where have you been these last fifteen years?"

"Here and there."

"In foreign parts?"

"Maybe," the old man shrugged.

"Ha!" Percy gave a shout of admiration. "Well, man, wherever you have been, they taught you caution. Or is that tongue of yours looser when you report to your master?"

"I have no master," the pot-man retorted, "save myself."

"And you do not work for Robert Cecil? You do not tell all you see and hear to him, eh?"

"Who is Master Cecil?" the old man feigned innocence.

"Ho! A wit, as well! A babe at its mother's breast knows Master Cecil. When did you return to England, man?"

The question was hurled without warning.

Now, thought the pot-man, is the time to get down to business. The men with whom he parried words were Romanists—he had recognised them as such the first time he'd served them. It hadn't taken him long either, to find out that one was Master Robert Catesby.

The other man, the older one with the stooping shoulders, was a Percy of Northumberland's ilk, a family of Romanists if ever there was one, despite the fact they served King James and outwardly conformed to the English mode of worship. So there was nothing to be lost now by ceasing to prevaricate.

"I came home to England three months ago on the *Gilly-flower*."

36

"The *Gillyflower*? One of Master Paris's packets?"

"Aye. How else would a man without a passport get a passage?"

He spoke calmly with no attempt at apology.

"You were in exile?"

"A self-imposed exile, sirs. I found myself in a situation that gave me no choice."

The two men waited, unspeaking. Presently the pot-man seemed to pull his thoughts together.

"I rose for Mary Stuart in my youth and for my pains was taken to the Fleet prison and sentenced to the axe. I escaped and when I was recaptured they took me before Walsingham. He said there was one who could die instead of me—his hair flamed red like mine—and that I could have my life if I would serve him."

"So you agreed to spy for Walsingham? You let another man die in your place?"

"I did."

He spoke without emotion.

"I was young and afraid and life is doubly sweet when a man is in fear of losing it."

"At least I commend your honesty, pot-man. What happened then?"

"I took on another name and went to live in York, not many miles from my old home. Walsingham saw to it I had a reasonable living and I spied on Romanists for him."

The men to whom the pot-man spoke fixed him with a look of settled disgust.

"By Our Lady, you are a loathsome creature!"

"I was, but it didn't last for long. Remember, I was young and my father was already in exile in France, stripped of his estates. I wanted to live, to have the chance someday to get back what was rightly mine. When I had become accustomed to the relief of still being alive, I decided the only thing to do was to work for two masters. So I spied for Walsingham and helped my fellow Romanists at the same time. When a man works for the Crown, he is privy to many secrets. I was often able to help those citizens of York who were still true to Rome."

"You played a dangerous game, Master Pot-man."

"Aye, and I was discovered and given no alternative but to flee the country. That," he shrugged, "was fifteen years ago and now Walsingham and Elizabeth Tudor are dead. I had hoped to petition King James for the restoration of my family estates."

"You risked a great deal to come back to England. Do you still have faith in King James's promises?"

"I do not. James Stuart runs with the hare and hunts with the hounds. I thought that for the sake of his mother he might show favour to those like myself who lost so much in her cause."

"There are many in a similar state to yours and you have my sympathy, Master—?"

Tom Percy shrugged.

"By what name shall I call you?"

"It is of no account now. I am of noble birth and once the heir to a manor and its title. But I was forced to take on another name when I worked for Walsingham. Both those names might be known to Cecil, for he inherited all that Walsingham set up. It is better that I am nameless. Some call me the man with the red hair—"

He laughed briefly and bitterly.

"—and it's a title that fits. I like it, in truth, for my red hair is all I have left now of the richness of my youth."

"And what will you do now, Master Potman-of-the-red-hair?"

"I don't know. My time may yet come. I may be able to help the cause and in so doing, help myself."

"Help the cause? Which cause?"

"I speak in riddles, sirs," the red-haired man shrugged, "but isn't there always a cause to fight for somewhere secret in every man's heart? When the time comes, I shall be waiting here, for I have nothing to lose and much to gain."

"And if the time does not come?"

"Then I still have had good reason for returning to England. I married a shrew of a woman. We lived in hatred of each other, but there was a child—a fair little maid we called Elizabeth-Mary. I should like to see my Beth once more. If I could do that, I'd be glad."

He picked up the empty tankards, well satisfied with his performance.

They would not be slow to understand. Master Percy served King James and Master Catesby, though poor, was of an influential Romanist family. The more friends a man gathered round him, thought the man with the red hair, the easier life could become.

"If there is nothing else, sirs?"

"No, we thank you." Robert Catesby held out his hand. "And God go with you, friend."

For a moment he sat deep in thought, then turning to his companion, he said softly,

"Mark the pot-man well, Tom. There is truth in what he has said. In every man's heart there is a secret cause. It would be well to remember the red-headed one, for as you said, he is one of us. Maybe some day, he'll be of use to the secret cause that lies in *our* hearts where we can recognise it for what it is."

He nodded to himself as if discovering a great truth.

"Aye, mark him well, I say!"

*   *   *

Anne Weaver sat in the light, airy solar listening to the

laughter of the children who played on the lawns below the open window.

There was a great deal to be said for being a grand-dam, she decided. It was, she was sure, the good Lord's compensation for advancing years.

But she had ceased to be a grand-dam many years ago if the truth were known, she reasoned, a frown creasing her brow into far away brooding. Still, the truth wasn't known so it didn't matter. There was, in fact, scarce anybody alive now who could have told Harry Weaver that the woman he called mother was his grand-dam and the girl who had borne him lay in a secret grave beneath Weaver's Oak at the crossing of the roads above the village.

"I'll give you a kiss for your thoughts, love."

John Weaver stretched his legs and smiled at his wife. "Only come over here for it, will you? I'm so weary I think I shall never get out of this chair again."

Anne rose painstakingly to her feet, cursing the rheumatism that even in the warmth of the July afternoon, plagued her constantly.

"I can't understand your need to have gone traipsing off to York in all this heat, husband. Why did you want to see the notary?"

John smiled, but there was a sadness about it.

"I don't rightly know, Anne. I think I have been meaning to see him ever since the Queen died. I suddenly came to realise how old I am. I wanted to settle one or two things regarding Harry's children. Young Diccon is provided for and Aldbridge will be his one day, but I had it in my mind to provide a better dowry for Jane and Margaret and set young Peter up with land of his own. And there is little Anna, now, to see to. It is a great responsibility, Anne, to have wealth."

"Aye, and I often wonder if we'd have been happier the way we were."

John reached up and patted the old hand that fondled his face.

"Tell me, wife, what you were thinking about with such an expression of concentration on your face."

"I was thinking of Harry's children and the joy we have had of them," she smiled. "And I thought too of Meg."

Anne sighed. They seemed to think a lot these days about Meg, but perhaps it was natural to hark back to the past when a body was getting old.

"How was York?" she asked, suddenly not wanting to think either of what had been or what was to come.

"It was hot, love, and it was so crowded I thought the city walls would split. I hadn't realised Queen Anna would be there."

Despite her dislike of the Stuarts, Anne asked, "What is she like, this new Queen?"

"I didn't see a lot of the lady. She went straight to her lodgings—no doubt she was tired—but what I saw pleased me. She is tall and slender; her eyes are blue and her hair is long and golden. She's a bonny woman, but sad."

"Aye, and she would be sad, married to a Stuart," Anne conceded.

"They said it is because she mourns her chrisom-child. Talk had it that she brought the dead babe with her in a tiny black coffin. Folks said she wouldn't leave the little body behind her in Scotland."

"I heard she was big with child when James Stuart set out for England. I am sorry for her, for even a Stuart must feel heartbreak at the loss of a child."

Anne sighed her sympathy, running her hands fondly through her husband's thin grey hair.

"I'll away and see Agnes Muff about the supper. Will a cold cut of meat suit you, John?"

"Aye, my lady, I am not hungry, I fear."

He smiled an apology, placing his hand to the back of his neck.

"Is there any balm in the potion-cupboard? I have a soreness behind my ear that feels like an insect bite."

Anne examined the redness at the back of John's neck, clucking indignantly as she did so.

"Why, by all that's holy, didn't you show it to me before? It's been a rare hungry insect to take such a bite at you, husband! Your neck is covered over with great red blotches. I'll wager one of those fat York fleas was responsible for it!"

Grumbling to herself about men who preferred pest-ridden city taverns to their own sweet and comfortable home, Anne went in search of the elder-flower lotion. Beth had just made a brewing from the new flowers of summer which would soon soothe away the ugly red weals.

She set her slow steps towards the laughter, for where there was the sound of children, so too could Beth be found.

"I'd be grateful, daughter, for some of your elder-flower lotion. Sir John has a sore neck. He swears it was caused by an insect bite, but it was a tavern flea that got at him, if you ask me!"

She held out her arms to the fat, chuckling baby.

"Here, give the little one to me and I will sit in the sunshine for a while. Be a good soul, Beth, and see to Sir John's neck for me?"

Beth settled the little Anna on the old woman's lap and like the dutiful daughter she was, sped off on her errand, a smile of contentment on her lips, her heart as light as a rising lark.

But she had not then seen the soreness on John Weaver's neck, and when laughingly she demanded that he take off his jacket and shake it from the window lest the fearsome flea should still be lurking there, still there was nothing on that exquisite day to make Beth Weaver's heart beat faster and her mouth to suddenly go dry; not until she saw the bright red rash that covered the whole of the old man's neck and seemed, almost as she watched, to spread to his arms and shoulders.

She said quietly, "Are you fevered, sir?"

She laid her hand on his forehead and was not surprised to find that it burned with heat.

"Don't you think you should rest a while on the bed? You have had a tiring couple of days—it is a long ride to York and back in this heat."

"No, Beth; I doubt I could sleep, for I can feel a terrible sweating coming on me. Perhaps I will walk to the parkland and find a cool spot under the trees."

He smiled.

"You have a healing touch, mistress; I feel better already for your ministrations."

But Beth was anxious as she helped her beloved Sir John to his feet. She had seen such a rash before and the remembrance of it made her afraid.

Then she shook herself mentally for her miserable forebodings. Sir John had had a nasty bite—probably it had become a little poisoned. There was nothing wrong that a marshmallow poultice wouldn't cure!

John Weaver leaned heavily on the gate, gazing over the parkland where red deer ran, grateful for the shade of the trees, wishing he did not burn so inside him.

With relief, he recognised the figure that strode towards him. Jeffrey Miller, his long-bow across his shoulder, raised his hand as he drew near.

"Bid you good-day, Sir John."

John felt an uplifting of his spirits as he always did when they met, for there was a safeness about Jeffrey, a steadfast quality John had come to rely on over the years. And Jeffrey who worked the corn-mill was more than a friend. He had loved Meg. Once they were pledged, but Meg had died and Jeffrey had married Judith.

John smiled into the open honest face as Jeffrey set down his bow.

"Are you not away to watch the archery practice, sir?"

Despite the coming of the dreadful gunpowder, men still practised their shooting as the laws of England demanded.

It was unusual, Jeffrey thought, that Sir John was not already down at the butts.

"Is something amiss, sir? Are you badly?"

He need not have asked; a glance at the flushed and sweating face told Jeffrey that all was not well with John Weaver.

"You are ill, Sir John. Let me help you home?"

"No, it is all right, save I fear I have caught a chill. I have sneezed so much that I ache."

He tried to smile reassurance, but inside him a dreadful fear raged.

"Can you spare a minute of your time, Jeffrey?"

Suddenly John wanted to talk. Deep within him he felt a need to set things to rights.

"I wouldn't ask it, but there are things I want to say to you for the sake of times past."

"It's no bother, Sir John. I was only going to shoot a little."

A feeling of unease washed over Jeffrey, but for all that he waited unspeaking for John to continue.

"You and I have known each other a long time Jeffrey, and I have good reason to be grateful for your loyalty. There is only yourself now, apart from Lady Anne and me, who knows about Harry's parentage. Soon you will be the sole keeper of his secret, for I think that by now the only other person who was privy to it must be long since dead."

"Pray to heaven he is!" echoed Jeffrey with cheerful practicality, "although he is only a little older than me and I'm good for a few years yet!"

Then, seeing the distress on the old man's face, he hastened, "Whether or not, sir, we shall not see *his* face in Aldbridge again. Remember, we sent him packing many years ago. He knows that if he came back, you or I could have him in Clifford's Tower for the traitor he is. He should have lost his head twice over!"

"You'd have killed him, wouldn't you Jeffrey, all those years ago? You'd have done for him . . . ?"

"That I would, sir. I'd have thought of Meg as I did it and felt no pity. It was only your charity that saved him."

"But if he should turn up again, after I'm gone?"

"I shall deal with him, never fear, and it will be my pleasure and my right, an' all. I do not hate easily, but . . ."

Then he slapped his thigh with his great strong hand.

"But why all this morbid talk, Sir John, on such a fine summer day? Tell me what causes your sadness?"

"I don't rightly know. Perhaps there is something inside a man that warns him when time is short and bids him do the things that needs be done."

John raised his head and in Jeffrey's eyes he read understanding and compassion.

"I think I am trying to thank you for being so true a friend, Jeffrey, and to ask you to watch over Harry when my time comes. Remember, he could have been your son . . ."

"More's the pity he wasn't although," he hastened, "I have a fine wife in Judith."

"And you called your only lass for Meg . . ."

"I loved Meg. The love I gave Judith was that of a grown man, but Meg was my first love and I shall never forget her. Even if I tried, I couldn't, for when the heartsease blooms afresh I feel an ache in my heart. I feel it for the boy I once was; I feel it for Meg and for what might have been."

Jeffrey was silent and lost in the past, then suddenly he threw back his head and laughed out loud.

"Sir John, with all respect, we must stop this mooning and be away to the butts. The day is too sweet to spend in regret. Come with me," he coaxed, "and let the fresh air blow away your sneezes and the hiss of arrows rid you of your ill-humour. What do you say?"

But John shook his head.

"No, friend. A rest in the cool of the trees is more to my liking this day."

He stopped, staring ahead of him, then he said, "Bear with me a little longer for there is something else . . ."

He lifted his shoulders as if suddenly coming to a decision.

"If at any time in the future you feel that Harry should know certain truths about his begetting, then I release you now from the oath of secrecy you swore to me when Meg died. If for some reason you cannot held your peace or if it happens that Harry should need to be told the truth of his parentage, you have my blessing to tell him. I know you would not take such a decision lightly."

He held out his hand and a gentle smile creased his face. It seemed to Jeffrey that the old man, having had his say, seemed the better for it. It was almost as if he was glad to ease the burden from his tired shoulders and hand it into another's keeping.

His hand felt frail inside that of the corn-miller's as he whispered, "God go with you, good Jeffrey."

CHAPTER FOUR

JEFFREY walked slowly away, wondering why John Weaver had spoken as he did. There had been a sadness about Sir John that defied his understanding.

The beck, when he reached it, was only a slow trickle and easy to cross by the broad, flat stones that stood high and dry in the summer months.

Meg once sat there, Jeffrey remembered. Before they were troth-plighted, when he had loved her shyly and from afar he had often seen her dreaming there. He had been proud and a little unbelieving when he and Meg were pledged, but their marriage had never been and it all seemed a long time ago now. Sometimes he still felt Meg was near him; it had been good to talk of her with Sir John, to recall the maid of the pale gold hair and the dreaming eyes. His youth had gone with Meg, Jeffrey brooded.

The night she died, calling not for him but for her lover, something in his heart had shrivelled and died with her.

Only at springtime when his blood ran hot as a youngling's and he remembered Meg, was he truly whole again.

She was near him today. He felt her presence in the air about him and heard her call in the warm summer breeze; she beckoned to him from the past, whispering from the secret places of his heart.

"Comfort him. He is old and afraid. If ever you loved me, Jeffrey, help him . . . ?"

He spun round, turned by invisible hands at his shoulders.

John Weaver was still there, leaning on the gate at the top of the rise. Then he held out his hand and the action seemed to Jeffrey to be so final, so full of pleading, that his mouth turned dry with fear.

"Jesu, I am a blind fool!" he spat and ran back towards the gate as if a life depended on it.

Anne Weaver saw their stumbling approach. With fear rising in her throat, she hobbled across the grass to where Jeffrey half carried the inert figure of her husband.

'I don't like it.'

Beth's words, spoken so short a time ago, came back to Anne, causing her breath to hiss sharply in her nostrils and a cold fear to tingle down her spine.

'I've seen a rash like that before . . .'

"What do you mean, Beth? Do you think Sir John is sickening for something?"

"I don't know, my lady—I couldn't be sure . . ."

Beth had been reluctant to voice her fears, but they had showed in her face and in her anxious eyes.

Now Anne felt a wave of nausea as she watched John's pathetic efforts to stay on his feet. She should have known. How could she have been so blind?

"Take Sir John to the winter-parlour," Anne whispered to Jeffrey as they stumbled up the steps to where the great doors stood open to the sunshine and Beth waited anxiously.

Anne watched her daughter-in-law's face as the truth of the situation was slowly becoming apparent.

"Sweet Jesus," Beth whispered, her eyes suddenly wide with fear.

"Aye," Anne nodded. "You suspected it all along, didn't you?"

"I think I did, but it didn't seem possible."

"Not possible when York is crowded to bursting point with

incomers and half of them from London to fawn upon the new Queen? Not possible when London is crawling with the plague?"

Beth closed her eyes, her face paper-white.

"The bite?"

"Aye, Beth, from a plague flea, carried from London and all because the Stuart Queen is in York!"

Anne Weaver's lips trembled.

"Hurry with that bed, can't you?" she spat as the horse-man and a stable-lad tugged and heaved a truckle bed down the staircase.

Behind them waddled Agnes Muff, her arms clasping a pile of blankets.

"There's hot coals ready for the warming-pan, my lady," she panted, "I'll bring it to you."

"No, Agnes, listen to me—and you, Beth. Once I have got Sir John into bed, the door is to be closed behind me. No one—*no one*—you hear me, is to come into that room!"

"But my lady, you cannot be alone!"

"I can, Beth, and for me it's a matter of no consequence. It is my right and my privilege to nurse my man. Anything I need can be passed in through the window and slops and such-like passed out. It'll be easier and safer and it won't be for long, one way or the other," she whispered, her lips stiff with fear, "for the sneezing has started already."

She was quiet for a moment, as if willing herself to believe the words she herself had spoken. Then she tilted her chin bravely.

"Now mind what I say, Beth. If you want me, you must tap on the window. And nail a blanket over the door . . ."

Anne's mouth trembled. It seemed almost that she was reluctant to enter the winter-parlour for once inside she knew she would be alone with a man who was almost certainly suffering from bubonic plague, the Black Death that raged in London. And most terrible of all, there was little she could do to help him.

"Mother of God be with me, for I am so afraid," she prayed, her hand on the latch of the door.

Reluctantly she raised it then, squaring her tired old shoulders, she walked quickly into the little room, the slamming of the heavy door behind her sounding like the crash of doom in her ears.

"There, now, all will be well, husband. We'll soon have that fever sweated out of you!"

John Weaver did not reply but mutely raised his eyes to those of his wife.

He had seen his hands. Already, the purple-black swellings were showing and his armpits throbbed painfully. Doubtless the swellings could be found there, too. Soon, he knew, he would be covered with suppurating sores and after that, the vomiting and the bleeding . . .

"Anne?" he whispered.

Even to say that beloved name was an effort. Desperately he fought the blackness that threatened to engulf him.

It was because of the flea-bite, he knew it, but he must not give in.

"Anne, love?"

"I am here, John."

Not caring about the angry swellings, she took his hand in hers and deliberately laid it to her cheek.

"I shall not leave you, dearest man."

Anne Weaver rose stiffly to her feet and ran her tongue round her dry lips. She shouldn't have fallen asleep, she thought, as she raised the candle above her husband's head.

"John?" she whispered, her lips to his ear.

But there was no reply.

For most of the night he had tossed and turned and

sweated, his body jerking in spasms of pain, his life-blood pumping from him each time he vomited.

Now he lay still, his breathing laboured, his face a distortion of putrid scabs.

Anne hobbled to the fire and threw cedar-wood and bay leaves and lavender flowers into the burning coals, for now the room was filled with the stench that heralded death.

On the bench by the bedside lay a dead toad. Barnabas had brought it. A toad caught in the moonlight at Lammastide, he said, and dried from the rafters of a church bell-tower, would cure even the most deadly dose of plague.

Anne had accepted the shrivelled offering, for the poor hunchback meant only to be kind, she knew. How quickly, she sighed, did bad news travel. Barnabas lived two miles down-river, yet in no time at all he was standing at the kitchen door, begging that Agnes Muff give the plague-charm to my lady that she might stuff it under the master's shirt.

Anne wondered if such faith and devotion could really bring about a little miracle. She had always scoffed at such fads, but now she wasn't sure.

She picked up the toad between the tips of her thumb and forefinger, looking at the face that was even more grotesque in death. It was, she thought, like one of the church gargoyles —ugly, beyond belief.

She sighed deeply. She was being foolish, but she could not—dare not—leave anything to chance.

Opening John's shirt, she laid the creature on his heaving chest. When one god failed, she thought grimly, there was nothing to do but try another.

She spun round guiltily as a soft insistent tapping on the window shocked her muddled thoughts into order again.

Carefully she wiped John's forehead and pulled the bed-sheet under his chin again before making her way stiffly to the window.

"Is it you, Harry?"

"No, my lady—it's Jeffrey."

"Ah, Jeffrey. You shouldn't have come; you need not have bothered."

"It's no bother, madam. I couldn't sleep, so I dressed myself and took a turn outside in the cool air. I met Mister Harry on his way to Ripon and I told him I'd stay within call until he got back."

"What time is it, Jeffrey? I fear I have slept a little."

"It wants but two hours to daylight. I'll stay here by the window until the young master gets back with the physician," he replied quietly, and Anne was grateful for his presence.

She did not know why she had sent Harry to Ripon, for it was almost certain that when he had heard a recital of John's symptoms, the physician would refuse to come. Either the patient would recover or he would die, the man would say. It was as simple and awful as that with the Black Death.

"How is Sir John?"

"He is very ill. He has tossed and muttered all night. Soon, I fear, I must send for the priest."

She shivered and hugged her shawl closer.

"I shall be glad when it is daylight, Jeffrey."

Anne didn't like the time before dawn, for it was during those lonely hours that a soul was most likely to leave its earthly body.

If John had to die, Anne prayed silently, could it not be in the daytime? Wouldn't she be better able to bear it if the sun was shining and the birds singing?

"You are cold, my lady. Close the window and build up the fire. I will stay here so that you do not feel alone."

Anne nodded her head and quietly closed the window.

Dear Jeffrey, she thought. Strong and enduring as an old castle keep. She was glad he was there, just the other side of the window-glass.

Sighing, she picked up a cloth and wiped her husband's brow again.

"I am here, John love," she whispered, but the man who lay in agony was too near to death to heed her words.

Anne lifted her eyes to the ceiling.

"Dear God, what will I do?" she pleaded. "How will I bear to be without him?"

Beth Weaver lay lonely and unsleeping in the large soft bed.

Without Harry, she thought, I am only half a person; an empty thing, needing his nearness to breathe life into me.

She moved her head angrily on the pillow.

"God's death," she whispered, "it is awful to be so helpless!"

She stared into the darkness, closing her ears to the rhyme that chanted itself through her head each time she closed her eyes.

> Ring a ring o' roses,
> A pocket full of posies,
> A tishoo! A tishoo!
> We all fall down!

She had sung it as a child, not understanding its terrible meaning, not knowing she would ever see the rash that resembled the petals of a red rose or that she would fearfully hang posies of herbs to sweeten away the evil stench of a plague victim.

She couldn't have known as she jigged to that rhyme that she would hear the sneezing that warned of death.

Sir John had been the first. Who next would fall a victim to the evil? Who next would start to sneeze?

The cathedral that stood guard over Ripon glowed palely

in the sunrise and Harry Weaver was glad to see its great comforting bulk.

Please God, the physician would be up and about, he thought, impatient to be back in Aldbridge. It would be all right, he told himself yet again; the physician would know what to do. People had been known to recover from the Black Death. If the disease didn't fell a man within forty-eight hours, it was said, then there was hope.

He dug his heels into his mare's sides, swinging to the left and down the narrow street towards the physician's house.

The serving-maid bobbed a curtsy in answer to his enquiry.

"I'm sorry, sir, but the physician's not at home. He's away to York selling potions and posies against the plague. Folk are going down like flies with it, so the master packed his bags and was off. 'A man mustn't let such an opportunity slip by', he said."

"No," Harry retorted sourly, "a man mustn't!"

He shrugged his shoulders. There was little else he could do. If he rode on to Thirsk he'd doubtless be greeted with the same story. Best he should get back home to his mother and Beth.

Wonderingly, he touched the back of his neck.

It could have been me, he thought. I could be lying there now, writhing in torment, looking into Beth's stricken face . . .

He turned dejectedly away as the door closed in his face. Unhitching the horses, he walked slowly to the top of the road, his eyes downcast, his shoulders bowed with despair.

"Sir. Oh, sir, come quick, I beg of you . . ."

A small frightened face looked up into Harry's, a small dirty fist tugged at his sleeve.

"In God's name, help us?"

"What is it, lad?" Harry asked gently, noting that the boy

54

was about Peter's age and build. No child of such tender years should look that afraid, he thought.

"What bothers you, lad?"

"It's the Pursuivants, sir. They are at the house and wanting more money. My mother has none and they will take away our pots and blankets!"

"By God, they shall not!" Harry Weaver's face flushed in anger.

"Where do you live, boy?"

"Up here, master. Hurry—my father is away and my mother is a-feared."

"Damn them!" Harry spat as he ran close on the heels of the barefoot child.

He hated the Pursuivants. They searched out Romanists in the name of England but feathered their own nests by accepting payment for their silence. Many Romanists paid regularly to keep the Pursuivants sweet, but once their money had gone, they had nothing to offer but their chattels. After that, destitute and afraid, they moved on yet again like hounded animals.

"Isn't there enough suffering in the world?" he whispered as he ran.

He had nothing against any Romanist—how they prayed was their own business. True, there were none in Aldbridge, but the north of England was still for the most part reluctant to abandon the old faith and many paid regularly and dearly for their beliefs.

"In here, sir."

The boy pushed open a door, then stood fearfully aside.

"Stop them? Please send them away?"

In a corner of the bare room a young girl sobbed pitifully and a woman stood over her protectively, her face set in fear.

"I beg you, don't molest the maid. She is pure—"

"Pure, eh? Ain't ever heard of a pure Romanist!"

55

The man's remark drew roars of coarse laughter from his companions.

"Come now, mistress, it's your wench or your chattels. Or shall we do our bounden duty and throw you into prison with your man? Take your pick!"

Harry Weaver's rapier whistled from its sheath.

"Damn you, fellow, it will be neither!" he spat.

The men whipped round, shocked into silence.

"Sir, we are servants of His Majesty. We seek out Romanists—enemies of England. We are about the King's business!"

"Does the King's business include the raping of a young girl? Does King James authorise you to cheat and steal for your own ends?"

There was a stunned silence, then the ugly ringleader spoke.

"What is your interest in this house, might I ask? It is obvious you are of the nobility—are you also a Romanist? I'd tread carefully if I wore your shoes. Aiding the King's enemies is treasonable!"

"And so is looting and raping in the King's name! By God, I could run you through for it if I'd a mind to!"

Almost blinded by rage, Harry Weaver reached out with his great hand and taking the man by the throat, propelled him to the door.

"Out with you, servant of King James! Be about your lawful business and leave womenfolk alone, else I'll have you clapped in prison soon as spit! *Out!*" he roared, aiming a kick at the retreating backsides.

He stood for a moment watching their ignominious flight, his shoulders heaving with anger.

"Damn and blast them!" he choked.

"And bless *you*, good sir. We heard there was a tussle. We were about to add our swords to yours!"

Harry spun round, his rapier still at the ready.

"Hold up, sir—we too dislike such scum. We were about to help this woman, but you beat us to it."

"Your pardon, friend."

He slid his weapon back into its sheath, eyeing the men who had joined him.

"I am Harry Weaver of Aldbridge and glad to be of service, sirs."

"Ha!"

The fair-haired of the two jumped from his horse, a grin on his lips, his hand held out in greeting.

"By Our Lady, I'd have known that red head anywhere. Don't you remember us? We sat in the same miserable schoolroom, time gone. Have you forgotten?"

"An' I recall you too, Harry Weaver."

Now the other man took up the baiting. "You were always being thrashed for playing truant. You preferred wenching to learning. What was her name? Beth, wasn't it?"

"I beg you, stop this teasing, for it is certain we were once well acquainted."

The fair-haired man bowed deeply.

"Christopher Wright of Pocklington, and this is Guy Fawkes who once lived in Petergate, in York. Have we changed so much?"

Harry gave a shout of recognition, glad, in his unhappiness, to laugh again.

"Well met, friends! It is good to see you again! How have you fared, these years past?"

"I have been helping to run the family estates—or what's left to us of them," Wright shrugged, "and Guy has been soldiering abroad."

Quizzically he eyed Harry Weaver.

"And you? It would seem you too have embraced the true faith or why should you set about Cecil's men?"

Harry Weaver shrugged.

"No, Christopher, I cleave to the English church, but first I am a Northerner and when I see a woman being hounded by Cecil's thugs, then my temper gets the better of me, I fear."

"Then I am right sorry," Fawkes replied gently, "for I thought you were of our faith. But for all that, I thank you for helping the poor woman. Your intervention will not set well with Cecil."

"Be damned to Cecil!" Harry growled. "London is a long way off and anyway, I am not in the habit of announcing myself when I kick a ruffian's backside down the street. The fellow doesn't know my name and he'll not be back, I reckon, to ask it!"

Turning to the woman he had helped, he said, "Hold out your apron, mistress," and opening his pouch, he emptied it into her lap.

"There is not a lot, but it will help feed you until your man is back."

"My husband is not a felon, sir. He is in prison because we can no longer pay our fines for non-attendance at church. He is a good man, but stubborn in his beliefs."

"Then pay your fines," Harry smiled, "that he may be released."

Tears misted the woman's eyes.

"God bless your goodness, sir. I will pray for you."

"Nay, mistress, I do not covet your prayers, but will you of your charity, light a secret candle for my father's sake? He is very ill and needs all your good intentions. Pray for John Weaver, I beg of you."

He held out his hand in turn to the friends of his youth.

"I dare not delay for my father is sick of the plague, but when happier times come again, you are both welcome at Aldbridge. By the way," he smiled, "the wench I was so often thrashed for—she has been my wife these sixteen years! Come to our home and meet her, eh?"

"We will, and gladly," Fawkes laughed, "but we too must go our separate ways. I'm for Scotton to see my mother."

"And I'm for Pocklington and home. My brother-in-law, Tom Percy, is expected there and I am anxious for news from London," Wright smiled. "I will pray for your father, Harry. May God go with you."

So, briefly met, the three old schoolfellows went their separate ways and all too occupied with other matters to give a second thought to Cecil's Pursuivants.

But the leader of that band of thugs had taken his defeat as a personal slight. Skulking by the street-midden, he watched the riders clatter off before slowly making his way towards the house from which he had been so painfully ejected.

The small boy sat on the pavement, his fears forgotten and all well with his child's world again. But his contentment was not to last as he raised his eyes and met those of his tormentor again.

The man did not attempt to touch him, but sat down beside him whispering softly.

"Do you want to earn a groat, lad? I've a coin here that is yours if you can tell me what those noblemen were talking about."

The shifty eyes glinted.

"I mean, lad, you can either tell me or I shall be back into your houseplace and I will beat your mother for the Romanist bitch that she is. Then I shall have my way with your virgin sister, after which I shall be ready for my breakfast!"

The thin lips parted in a leer of black, broken teeth and he thrust his face near that of the child.

"And do you know what I eat for breakfast, boy? I eat

Romanist lads! I cut 'em into little pieces and sprinkle 'em with holy water and I gulps 'em down!"

A hand shot out and grasped the boy's hair.

"So you're going to be a sensible lad, aren't you . . . ?"

*   *   *

The sun was warm as Harry Weaver's mare clattered over the brow of the hill and came upon the crossroads by Weaver's Oak.

Pulling hard on the reins, he wheeled the creature to a stop, straining his ears to catch a sound he did not want to hear.

He waited, counting the seconds. Perhaps he had been wrong, he thought, relaxing his shoulders again, letting go his breath with a hiss of relief.

But then it came again, borne sadly on the breeze and there was no more denying it; no denying who had died.

Barnabas was at his work again, tolling the sombre-sounding bell that helped a soul's passing.

Like a man half asleep, Harry Weaver walked slowly to the lonely tree that men knew as Weaver's Oak. It was planted, his mother once said, partly as a pledge and partly for Meg that her lonely grave might be protected.

Now, whenever he passed it, Harry thought, he would remember not only Meg but the man who long ago planted it; John Weaver, by the grace of Elizabeth Tudor, lord of the manor of Aldbridge. John Weaver, husband and father; slow to anger, quick to forgive. John Weaver, who was dead of the plague.

For the first time since his boyhood, when Diccon Miller had died in his arms, Harry wept.

But there was elation in the heart of the pock-marked Pursuivant called Beelzebub as he sat, pen trimmed, in the tavern in the market place at Ripon. True, he conceded, he had been cheated of one prize that day, but how much more profitable would this information be? Robert Cecil paid well for such succulent little snippets to add to his records. Cecil was strong and powerful and he had become so by knowing who his enemies were.

Well here, gloated the man whose eyes shone with the cunning of an old dog-fox, were three more enemies Cecil should know about!

Guy Fawkes, gentleman, once of Petergate, York; Christopher Wright, gentleman, of Pocklington in the county of York; and Harry Weaver, nobleman, of the manor of Aldbridge—Romanists; defenders of Romanists; enemies of England!

CHAPTER FIVE

1604

THERE was no moon and the April night was dark and soft as black velvet.

The two men walked with the stealth of prowling cats, their eyes shifting warily, the younger of them uneasy, doubting the wisdom of his actions in following the man who had knocked on the door of his lodgings at the *Red Bull* tavern.

"My master presents his compliments and asks that you follow me to his house."

"And why should I, fellow?" the young man shrugged, fixing the messenger with his pale blue eyes.

"What is your master's name and what business can he and I have?"

And why, he pondered, does he set the hour of our meeting at a time when most men are safely behind their barred and bolted doors?

"Sir, the one I must not tell you; the other, I do not know. I am here to carry a message and to tell you if you have any doubts that once at the palace of Escorial, you met an old schoolfellow. That man's brother is one of those you will meet tonight. You will be with friends."

He had met Christopher Wright at Escorial, the man mused.

"And what do you know of me?" he demanded, intrigued. "Did he tell you my name, this mysterious master of yours?"

"I know nothing of you, sir, but I was told to ask—

discreetly, you understand—the whereabouts of a Master Fawkes."

"Then you have the better of me, for I do not know you."

"My name is Bates. I serve the one who sent me and I see nothing and know nothing. Have no fear of me."

So Master Fawkes had taken his pistols from the chest beneath his bed and belted on his rapier. He was not a swordsman, despite his profession, but a sword and spurs gave a man prestige.

Fawkes was a powderman; he excelled in the new and deadly way of killing. Let yeomen cleave to their long-bows; soon, he knew, such weapons would be things of the past.

"Where now?" he whispered as they left Drury Lane.

"To the *Irish Boy*. I have horses waiting at the stables there; it's only a spitting distance now to the Strand."

Horses? The man lived out of London then, Fawkes reasoned. But a shrugging of his shoulders was the only reply the taciturn servant gave when asked.

A scavenging dog slunk along the gutter and here and there a chink of light showed through window screens. In the distance a watchman called the hour, his voice lonely in the still and shuttered city. Few lights burned at doorways; few honest men stirred from the warmth of their hearths.

The gutters stank and the men walked in the middle of the roadway, reluctant to tread carelessly into the slime of rotting food and rubbish and dung.

"We will walk the horses a little way, sir," Bates whispered. "No sense in kicking up a fuss."

So quietly they left the warren of streets behind them and smelled the clean sweet air again. Their horses were fresh and eager for a gallop, speeding between hedgerows, sure-footed in the darkness.

At a crossroads by a cluster of cottage dwellings, they slowed their mounts to a walk.

"There's Uxbridge ahead of us, Master Fawkes. My master lives a little beyond it. Best we should walk the horses again . . ."

The night sky was clear now and pricked with stars and in the distance Fawkes' eyes picked out the shape of a house, sombre and lonely, its sloping roof and twisted chimneys stark against the starlight.

Bates nodded his head.

"The house of my master," he said.

From the darkness of an archway, an ostler silently reached out for the bridles of their horses, leading them away without speaking.

Ahead of them a door opened.

"Welcome to Moorcrofts, friend Fawkes," whispered a strange voice.

There was no going back now.

*　　　*　　　*

Anne Weaver rested in the shelter of the thick evergreen hedge and wished she had not strayed so far from the comfort of her chair.

To arrive triumphantly at the farthest end of the yew-walk was one thing; to have to walk back was quite another, she thought irritably. But she was old now, too old and missing John almost unbearably. She had sat alone in the winter-parlour until she could bear it no longer, and bringing down her cane with a determined thump, rose painfully to her feet, suddenly needing to be out of the small, intimate room in which John had died so horribly.

She wanted to escape from the loneliness of the present and be with John and Meg once more. She wanted to be a yeoman's wife again with strong arms, a straight back and nothing worse to worry about than Meg's eternal dreaming or the brown hen a wild cat killed.

She had thought hopefully that the April sun might have coaxed the heartsease into bloom and was disappointed to find it was not so. The tiny flowers seemed reluctant still to lift their faces as if even they were determined to refuse Anne the comfort she so desperately craved.

The heartsease had been Meg's flower; she had embroidered them round the neck of the first dress of her womanhood and not long after they had pulled that dress over her lifeless body . . .

Anne shook her shoulders and straightened her back.

She must not think of the way Meg died for to do so still filled her heart with bitterness. Meg had been the first of the innocents sacrificed in Mary Stuart's name. Meg had been falsely accused to ensure her silence.

"She is a witch, I say!"

Poor little wench, denounced by her lover, and all for Mary Stuart's sake.

Now John was dead, his beloved body a mass of stinking sores so that even Anne herself had puked to look on him.

If only, Anne reasoned for the thousandth time, the Stuart Queen had not been in York, luring every plague-infected scrounger from the south! Always it was a Stuart who spawned trouble. Would she never be free of their mischief, Anne fretted. She hated and feared them as she hated and feared the devil.

And there would be a Stuart at the bottom of the trouble that was to come, she reasoned. And trouble was coming. She could scent it as a hound scented a stag. It made her heartbeats quicken and it smelled foul in her nostrils.

Since John died, she had tried to be mindful of her blessings and grateful that no one else had taken the fearful disease. It could have been Beth or one of the children; it could have swept through Aldbridge like a rampaging gale . . .

But it didn't help to count blessings when an old woman's

heart ached to breaking point; when none of it need have happened if it hadn't been for a Stuart.

Anne hugged her pain to her, rocking back and forth in misery and self-pity.

It was all because of the heartsease, she argued petulantly. She had been certain that if she looked beneath the yew-hedge she would find one flowering in a sheltered pocket and finding one would have been a sign from the Almighty that John was happy with Meg again.

She had been so sure she would pluck the first tender blossom of spring that she had decided to place it beneath her pillow and dream of times long gone; times when they had been a family, poor and happy and hard-working; sometimes hungry, sometimes sad, but a family for all that.

A tear trickled down the tired lines of her face and she left it unheeded to fall on her hand.

She had only asked the Almighty for a a small crumb of comfort to ease the bleak despair that wrapped her constantly around.

She raised her tear-drenched eyes to the sky.

"Sweet Jesus, why did you not take me, too? Why have you left me here?"

She shook her head despairingly, trying to remind herself that she must never ask God for a reason, even though He saw fit to deny her just one little flower.

"Oh, John, my dear love," she whispered.

She heard the crunch of a footfall and closed her eyes against the tell-tale tears. Tears were a private thing, she urged, dabbing her eyes and blowing her nose a little too noisily.

She looked up to see the miller's great comforting bulk towering above her.

"Oh, it's you, Jeffrey," she sighed, relief flooding over her, for Jeffrey would not scold as Harry did or fuss like Beth when she gave way to tears. He would not ask questions or try to jolly her into a happier frame of mind.

He understood, for he had been close to John—there was no need for play-acting with Jeffrey Miller.

"I was weeping," Anne admitted flatly. "I was missing John and wondering why God didn't let me die too. I'm an ungrateful old woman, Jeffrey. I reckon I'm so pesky that the Almighty doesn't want me."

Tenderly Jeffrey took the old hand in his.

"I reckon he doesn't, my lady," he said comfortingly. "There's a time for us all and yours hasn't come yet, nor mine. There must still be things left for us to do, I'm thinking."

"Aye, Jeffrey, but I fret for John for all that."

"Then would it help, my lady, to talk to me of Sir John? I loved him too, remember?"

"Yes, and he thought of you as a son, almost."

Anne patted the hand that lay beside hers.

"He looked upon you as kin, Jeffrey."

She swallowed painfully.

"But it isn't only my John I want to talk about. It's something I cannot explain—something that has me affeard. It would have been all right, you see, if John had been here. He'd have set things to rights or sorted out my foolishness."

"Then tell me, my lady?"

Anne shook her head.

"I cannot Jeffrey, not rightly. I cannot put it into words, but I can feel it all around me. There is mischief afoot, I am sure of it. It is so evil that sometimes I feel sick to my heart."

"So bad?"

"Aye, it is."

Jeffrey Miller felt a somersaulting at the pit of his stomach. Lady Anne was a down-to-earth woman with never a frivolous breath in her body.

"Could it be, my lady, that you have perhaps been shut up too long with your grief? Don't you think that now the spring herbs are growing, it might set well if you were to brew yourself a potion to cleanse your body of the evils of winter? Or perhaps you could take a glass or two of wine? They do say that wine is a fine medicine."

Anne shifted irritably.

"No, Jeffrey, it's not a malady of the body, though heaven knows I'm a poor old thing, now. No," she sighed, "this thing is in my mind like a rotten canker. I am no seer. I cannot look into the future, but I know there is evil about and it will cause a great upset in this house."

"Then I beg of you, put such thoughts from your mind, for today I found the antidote to all evil. I came especially to give it to you."

Anne looked up sharply.

"You've found *what*, Jeffrey Miller? Don't you know I don't believe in luck-charms?"

"This is no charm, my lady," Jeffrey's eyes teased gently. Then his face became serious again.

"I am sure Sir John would have wished it, for it was always his custom, I know. I thought this year he'd have wanted me to do it for him."

He smiled, then fumbled in the pouch at his belt.

"Hold out your hands . . ."

He dropped the tiny flower into Anne's entwined fingers.

"There you are, sweet my lady—the first heartsease. I found it at the cross-roads and thought you would like to have it."

"Oh, Jeffrey," Anne choked, tenderly holding the little flower to her face. "Dear friend, you cannot know how happy this makes me."

Tremulously she smiled up at him. He couldn't have known how desperately she had wanted to find a heartsease, yet he had sought her out in her misery and dropped one into her eager hands.

Something, *someone*, had told him of her need.

John must have whispered, ". . . *Take my Anne a heartsease, Jeffrey, that it might ease her aching heart . . .*"

She raised her eyes to the sky, the love and peace in them a thing of near-beauty.

"Help me to my feet, Jeffrey, and give me your arm. We will walk back to the house together, dear friend."

How foolish she had been, how untrusting of God's wisdom, Anne thought as they slowly trod the grass in the direction of the old house that glowed warm in the pale sunlight.

She must forget her foolish fears and cease tormenting herself, she resolved with fierce determination, glancing down at the tiny flower in her cupped hand.

She had been worrying, she was sure, over nothing more than an old woman's foolish fancies.

"*Oh, please God,*" she prayed silently, "*and let them have been only foolish fancies?*"

*   *   *

"With respect, your Majesty, I tell you it is no foolish fancy and I am not acting like an old woman!"

Robert Cecil unhooked his reading glasses and set them carefully on the table beside him.

"I desire only your Grace's well-being . . ."

"Aye, Robbie, my busy little beagle, so you do an' all and we are mindful of it," acknowledged James Stuart, "only don't go on so about it, man. It upsets my digestion, I say; it upsets my digestion!"

And it'll be more than thy royal belly that suffers if my fears are founded, the little hunchback thought wearily.

"Sire, I have no wish to alarm you. Indeed," hastened Cecil, "I am here to ensure that no harm comes to your royal person. But reports tell daily of growing unrest. Romanists are sickened at having to pay Recusancy fines again. My observers in the north of England tell me there is great unrest there."

"Then the Romanists must learn that they would do better to worship in *my* church, Robert, and place their pennies on *my* plates," the King retorted comfortably, supremely confident in the Almighty's divine protection.

"Don't fash yourself, man; do as I do, and have faith. Heaven protects the right!"

Maybe so, whispered Cecil's reason, but the trouble was that every man thought himself to be in the right.

Foolish man that James Stuart was, he fumed; never able to see the wood for the trees; incapable of heeding what was under his very nose, so intent was he upon his pleasures.

Fawn upon him, thought Cecil maliciously, admire him, shower him with gifts and he would purr like a cat at a cream jug. Fill him with wine, give him a pretty pageboy to lean on, sit him on a fast horse and England, aye, and Scotland too, could go to the devil for all James Stuart cared.

But his mother had been the same, hadn't she? Wilful and pleasure seeking, believing utterly in the divine right of those of the blood royal.

"Isn't that so, Robbie? I say, doesn't heaven take care of the righteous?"

Robert Cecil shut down his thoughts, treasonable to a high degree.

"Your Majesty is always right," he spluttered, trying hard to collect his ruffled composure.

"Then save your worries, Master Secretary, for more important things and your puff for cooling your porridge."

James smiled placatingly and Robert Cecil had cause to be grateful that he was no longer young, that his back was misshapen and his skin no longer soft and pink.

"And don't worry over much about the north country, Robbie, my dear."

The King of all Britain stroked the hand of his Principal Secretary, "for they're loyal to Scottish Jamie in York. You'll mind I gave a wee favour here and there on my way south—they like me in York; they like me."

A wee favour? Cecil almost exploded. *Here and there?*

By Our Lady, the man had thrown knighthoods around in York like a man with two pairs of busy hands! Then he'd sat back drooling and counted his Yorkshire gold!

How Cecil wished the King would take himself off again. If he couldn't be bothered to rule Britain, why couldn't he leave it entirely to someone who could; himself, for instance, Cecil thought fretfully.

Dear Lord, he mused, for how long did I scheme and plot to make sure that England's throne should not go to a Papist?

Elizabeth Tudor had often been a sore trial; he had never achieved the same easy relationship with her as Burghley, his father, had done.

There were times, Cecil admitted, when Elizabeth Tudor had driven him almost to distraction with her woman's wiles. But her little finger had cared more for England than the whole of James Stuart's body could ever do.

England had been the old Queen's passion, her joy and her despair.

But of one thing Robert Cecil was certain. He would give a great deal for the old days to come back again, despite Elizabeth Tudor's cantankerous ways.

But they wouldn't come back and now England was ruled by James Stuart who had nothing in common at all with his kinswoman, save for the fact that each of their mothers had lost her head for being foolish—and getting caught at it!

Cecil glanced up from his papers as the door slammed, thankful to be alone again, grateful that for all his aura of godliness, James Stuart was not yet able to read mens' minds. Had that been so, sighed the weary little man, this day he'd have lost his head thrice over for treasonable thoughts!

He shook his head in despair, remembering again. Elizabeth Tudor had always listened to advice. She'd not have run off to her pleasures and left another to settle the hash of the Romanists.

At least, he thought petulantly, she would have taken the time to read the report he had so painstakingly prepared.

He looped his glasses round his ears again and took up his quill. The old Queen would have been shocked and hurt to read that report.

The name of Christopher Wright she might well have known, for the Wrights at both Ploughlands and Pocklington were known Yorkshire Romanists. Ursula, their mother, had spent many years in prison for her faith.

"And who, Robin, is this Master Fawkes?" Elizabeth Tudor would have asked, most likely. "And what mischief was he up to in Ripon, think you?"

She would have remembered Ripon and the men of that city who joined Mary Stuart's cause.

But what would the fiery Tudor have thought to the third name mentioned in that report? Wouldn't her blood have run cold at the very sight of it?

Harry Weaver, gentleman, son of Sir John of the manor of Aldbridge.

Elizabeth's blood apart, thought Cecil, his own hadn't exactly warmed to the news. He would have staked his life on the unswerving loyalty of the Weavers. To learn that young Harry Weaver seemed at the very least to have Romanist sympathies, had been a very disquieting experience.

But the agent in the north who had long since sent the report, was a reliable man and not given to wild theories.

Cecil studied the white feather of his quill. If his memory

served him rightly, it had been in his father's time that John Weaver had been granted the title and lands of Aldbridge—a just reward, seemingly, for loyalty to Elizabeth Tudor at the time of the uprising in Yorkshire.

Damn them, those wild Northerners! Why did they cause so much bother?

Tomorrow, he decided, he would write to York and waken the men who sat on the Council of the North from their self-satisfied slumbers!

Testily he picked up the small silver bell at his side and rung it with unnecessary ferocity.

"What do we know of John Weaver and Harry, his son?" he enquired of the man who answered his summons. "Theirs is the manor of Aldbridge in Yorkshire—in the Northern Riding, I believe?"

Cecil allowed himself a brief moment of self-congratulation, for if there was anything at all to be known about the Weavers, it would have been noted.

If the landlord of the Bear Tavern at Southwark cut his toenails, Robert Cecil would know it.

"And when you've seen to that, Master Munck, see what we know about Master Guy Fawkes, of Scotton."

The days, it seemed were not long enough for Robert Cecil. Indeed, had the Almighty seen fit to endow that man with a body to match the boundless scope of his brain, He would have created a creature of near-perfection.

The little hunchback sighed.

Praise be that someone was caring for the Stuart's kingdom for him, for it seemed, he thought, as he poked reflectively at his teeth, that it certainly needed caring for.

God's death, he pondered uneasily, when a Weaver of Aldbridge turned his coat, anything was possible!

CHAPTER SIX

IT WAS strange, thought Guy Fawkes, that the warm May evening should suddenly turn chill and the lingering red of the twilight so quickly shift to night. Had it not been for the dim light of the waning moon, a man could be forgiven for thinking he was walking soft-footed into blackest hell.

But the house behind St. Clement's Inn was once a lodging-house for slaughtermen and Butcher's Row in which it stood had been a street of slaughter-houses. Small wonder then, that the high, narrow building should have an air of desolation about it.

The door of the lonely house opened slowly and Robert Catesby's servant squinted into the darkness.

"Give you greeting, friend," Fawkes whispered. "I am expected . . . ?"

"Aye, sir, and welcome."

Thomas Bates closed the door softly behind them.

"All are present now, Master Fawkes," he replied as he pushed home the heavy creaking bolts.

The empty house stank of decay, the floor-slabs in the passageway slimy with decomposing filth.

But the room into which Fawkes was ushered was excessively hot, for a fire burned in the hearth and candles flickered on either side of the mantelshelf. The two small windows had long ago been boarded up and very little air could enter the room nor any tell-tale light escape.

The men who had been at Moorcrofts leaned against the

walls and chimney breast, for the houseplace was empty of furniture.

The memory of Moorcrofts was still fresh in Fawkes' mind. It had been good to kneel before a priest of the true faith once more. He had left the house cleansed and uplifted like a man grown tall as a tree.

He wondered if the gentle little priest would again be there but a quick glance at the now-familiar faces sent his hopes tumbling.

"Well met, gentlemen," he greeted them softly.

"Welcome friend," Robert Catesby replied. "Now we can begin our business."

He cleared his throat noisily and instantly an air of expectant quiet pervaded the room.

"I would ask you all to remember that you are still bound by the sacred oath you swore before one of God's anointed priests and remind you that it is binding until death . . ."

Catesby's eyes ranged slowly round the room, to be answered by gazes steadfast as his own. Then he continued quietly, "I think, good sirs, that the time for talking and hoping is past. We are ruled by a weak and pleasure-seeking King who is nothing better than clay in the hands of the man who helped him to England's bounty. Robert Cecil is our sworn enemy and Robert Cecil," he whispered, "must be killed!"

There was a moment of shocked silence, then John Wright, who had gazed long and moodily into the glowing coals, asked bluntly, "How would that help our cause? There'd be another to take his place afore his bones were set in death!"

"Aye, Rob, he's right!"

"And how would you get near bossy little Robert, eh? He's guarded better'n the King."

"Ha! He's got more enemies than the King!"

"Get to him? It would be easy. What would you say if I

told you," Catesby continued persuasively, "that in doing for Cecil we could also be rid of Scottish Jamie and his Queen and any of the royal brats who might get in the way? What would you say to that, my friends?"

"I'd say," Thomas Winter replied quietly, "it was well-nigh impossible."

Robert Catesby smiled gently and dangerously.

"Oh, but you are so wrong, Tom, for it is not impossible. Indeed, with a little help from Guy here, we can accomplish just that."

"Me?" Fawkes coloured with pleasure. "How can I be of service, Master Catesby? I am not a rich man; I have no influence in high places—indeed, I am a gentleman of fortune, living on my wits and my skill as a soldier."

"Aye, and there you have it," Catesby interrupted triumphantly, *"your skill as a soldier, Guy!"*

"You mean with the powder?" Fawkes jerked. "Use gunpowder? But how in the world could it be done?"

"Think of Kirk o'Fields, gentlemen. Remember that less than forty years ago the Stuart's father was just so killed. How much better could we do it in the face of forty years' experience?"

"But *how* is it to be done?" John Wright persisted. "Is it likely, gentlemen?"

"It is more than likely!"

Catesby paused, smiling tantalisingly.

"They will come, all of them of their own accord, to where we shall be waiting and we shall shake England to her very foundations, I tell you!"

"I'm in no mood for riddles, Rob Catesby. Come to the point," Thomas Winter replied sharply.

"Very well, I will tell you. We will blow up Cecil and the King and anyone else who gets in our way. Next time they are all assembled, it will be easy!"

"Blow them up?"

"Talk sense, man! Where?"

"Aye, and what with? Powder is hard to come by. Do we present ourselves at the Tower and demand powder?"

"Ha! Gunpowder in the name of the King, for we seek to blow up the King!"

There was a roar of derisive laughter and then a silence, uncertain and disbelieving.

"*Can* it be done?"

"It can and it *will*!"

Now Thomas Percy spoke. Silent throughout, his eyes had moved from face to face as Catesby spoke, sizing up the reactions of his fellows, gauging their enthusiasm, measuring their disbelief.

"What Rob says is possible, I tell you. Forget about the gunpowder for the moment, for it may well be easier come by than you imagine."

Now Winter and Wright and Fawkes were silent. Percy had a persuasive tongue; he was easy to listen to.

"You ask *where* it can be done and I will tell you. When next Parliament assembles for the King's opening—there is the place. You seek to know *how* it can be done—it is only a matter of placing gunpowder beneath the floor of the chamber. *When*," Percy shrugged, "is a matter for the King and Cecil to decide. As soon as they know, so shall we. Then we can start counting the days to our freedom and heaven and all persecuted Catholics will bless us for it!"

* * *

The clerk who worked in Robert Cecil's private rooms tapped on his master's door.

"Lord Carew is asking to see you, my lord, on a matter of some urgency.

"Carew, eh?"

Cecil snapped shut the book he had been writing in and blinked his aching eyes. He would have to see him, for Carew was Lieutenant General of Ordnance and a trusted servant of King James; his domain was the Tower arsenal. Dedicated to his work, zealous to a fault when it came to the safe-keeping of the powder and weapons in his charge, Carew knew his job backwards and carried it out with assurance. Therefore, decided Cecil, an urgent request from such a man meant exactly what it implied.

"I will see him," he nodded, rising stiffly to his feet, "and see to it we are not disturbed, Munck."

He hoped Carew's visit would not be a long one, for there was much work still to be done.

He shrugged his misshapen shoulders. He was weary—tired of ruling in the King's stead; weary of scheming and conniving that he might stay one jump ahead of those who sought to bring him down; weary of looking over his shoulder for Jesuits dedicated to his extermination.

He sighed, taking two goblets and filling them with wine. He had long ago learned that when a man chose to sup with the devil, he needed a long spoon.

Let them snigger, then, as he passed; let them dub him Bossy Little Robin; let them make their feeble jokes about the King's tame beagle—no matter. He, Robert Cecil, had the longest spoon in Christendom and what was more, he knew how to sup from it!

He forced a smile as his visitor entered, offering him wine, motioning him to a seat.

"I'll not take up over much of your time, my lord," Carew settled himself, "for what I have to tell may be anything or nothing. It is only these days a man must protect himself and," he hastened, "his friends."

Cecil did not speak. He was a good listener. He had

learned over the years that a sympathetic ear could often achieve more than bribery and far more than threats.

"I mind, you see, that some who are around His Majesty are false. They sing his praises in public then privily sing their masses. There is one gentleman I have long suspected of such behaviour and one who may go to the devil for all I care, provided he leaves me alone. But when that man pokes his nose into my business, I don't like it."

Carew paused, seeking a crumb of encouragement.

"Indeed, my lord, and quite rightly too," Cecil murmured, nodding approval.

"So when this fellow deliberately seeks me out and begs a position in my employ for a friend of his—a trustworthy man, he says, fallen on hard times—I feel I must clear my own conscience and acquaint your lordship with the facts of the matter."

Robert Cecil drummed his fingers on the arm of his chair.

"The man's name?" he asked quietly.

"It's Tom Percy, and I don't need the wisdom of Solomon to know *his* inclinations!"

"So Master Percy begs a favour of you? There must be many who beg favours."

"Maybe so, but usually Papists beg favours from their own kind—why, then, from me?"

"Why indeed? Have you asked to meet this man?"

"I have already seen him—that was when I became uneasy, for this man is not one of the working classes, in spite of his being employed in a humble capacity at the *Irish Boy.*"

"Ah, yes, the *Irish Boy,*" Cecil whispered, half to himself.

"There's breeding in him, my lord, and arrogance that makes a mockery of his humble clothes."

"Then what would you take him for, my lord?"

"I'd say he was one of noble blood who has fallen on

hard times and these days a gentleman falls on lean times only if he has been indiscreet or careless with his inheritance—"

"Aye," nodded Cecil, "or if he has been relieved of that inheritance because of his indiscretion."

Their eyes met in mutual understanding, then Cecil placed his fingertips together and regarded them carefully.

"I think you should give work to this man, Carew. Find him a position in the Arsenal."

"The *Arsenal*, my lord?" Carew exploded.

"Just so," came the calm reply. "It is obvious that this is what Master Percy has in mind, so let him have his way."

"But Percy is a Romanist, for all he waits upon the King and attends prayers in the English Church!"

"I know it, Carew, and so does King James."

"Then why . . . ?"

"Because I ask it of you, friend. Have no fear; the responsibility will be mine."

"But if this potman is one of Percy's friends, it makes the whole matter very suspect."

"Exactly—and I am always suspicious. To me," Cecil replied comfortably, "every man is my enemy until I have proved him otherwise."

"Then what must I do?"

"Nothing, save to send a note to Percy. Tell him you could have given work to his unfortunate friend, but you fear that since all you can offer is in the Arsenal and dangerous and unhealthy work, you are sorry not to be able to help him. I'll lay odds," Cecil permitted himself a smile, "that before you know it, Percy and his man will be hammering on your door for the job, in spite of the danger. We shall know then, what to do."

"And then?"

"You will take on not only Percy's man but another also— I will acquaint you with his name later. He will be in *my* employ, Carew, and all he need do will be to watch the pot-man. See that my man has all the scope he needs. If you do that, you need not worry further. As I said, the responsibility will be mine, so what say you?"

For a moment the custodian of the King's gunpowder did not reply and Cecil could almost read his thoughts. Carew was suspicious of the whole thing, regretting already that he had not sent Tom Percy and his protégé packing without giving the matter a second thought.

"I am not happy about it, my lord," he muttered uneasily. "Surely, if this man's motives are in any way suspect, he should be given short shrift?"

"What—and miss the opportunity of letting the sprat catch us a mackerel—or a whale?"

"Surely it could not be so serious?"

"We must hope not, but we must be vigilant too, for we live in troublesome times when every man must scratch for himself."

"So I am to take on Tom Percy's man and another that you'll later acquaint me of?"

"Exactly. And when you have done that, you need not give the matter another thought. You were right to come to me, my lord, very right and sensible. I want to know more about this man; you didn't tell me his name."

"I doubt the name he gave me was the one he was born with, but it was Woodhall—Cedric Woodhall. He spoke with a strange tongue. Oh, I'd say he's English-born, but has lived amongst foreigners. There were one or two turns of phrase that put me in mind of the French."

"So! An Englishman come home from exile, maybe?"

Cecil took up his pen and reached for paper.

"What else can you tell me?"

"I'd say he had roots in the north country and at a guess, he'd be of late-middle years, fifty to sixty, maybe. I couldn't be sure, you see, for he had a good head of hair and that can be deceiving. It was red as a fox's pelt and curly."

Lord Carew paused.

"I didn't notice any more," he shrugged. "I'd have taken greater care if I'd known that it would be of such interest to you. I could try to find out more when next he comes to the Tower."

"No, Carew! That would make him suspicious. A Lieutenant-General does not bother himself with underlings. Give him the job then forget him; my man will take care of his comings and goings. You have done well in what you have told me so far."

"I have, my lord?"

"Indeed, friend. You have told me that this man Woodhall is a nobleman, most likely a Romanist who for some reason has found it expedient to live abroad. He is now associating with other Romanists. We also know that someone, somewhere, is in need of gunpowder."

And it wasn't only the matter of gunpowder either, he thought. Only yesterday, John Whinniard had been approached by Thomas Percy and asked for the tenement that was leased to Ferrars. At the time it had not seemed of special significance, but now, in the light of Carew's visit, it took on a different complexion, for the house Percy wanted butted onto Parliament House.

Now, it seemed, Percy was seeking gunpowder. Add to that the fact that Percy was a Romanist and the cauldron of intrigue started to bubble.

Robert Cecil trembled and his heart thudded. There was a tingling at the top of his spine that warned of danger. He had, he supposed, an inbuilt sense; an instinct he never ignored. That instinct told him now that something was hatching and it filled him with an elation that made him feel slightly tipsy. He loved a good game of wit-pitting, the more so if he played it with Papists; especially so since he was already one jump ahead of his opponent.

Stupid Thomas Percy to pick on the house that was occupied by Ferrars, one of the quiet men who watched and waited in the shadows. How careless of Percy to imagine that a house so near the seat of Government would be let to anyone who was not utterly trustworthy. But then, Percy was a fool; any man was a fool who thought he could hoodwink Robert Cecil!

He walked to the door of the small inner room where faithful Munck worked.

"I need some books from the privy vault," he said, handing over a large iron key. "Bring me the ones marked with the letter 'W'."

Cecil smiled benignly.

"By the bye, did you make a note of Lord Carew's visit?"

"I did, my lord. I have only to add the time at which he left."

His clerk, Cecil decided, was becoming most efficient at his job. Levinus Munck worked solely for Cecil and was paid out of Cecil's own pocket. He wrote quickly and with a good hand and had been fast to learn the importance of seemingly useless scraps of information. He had a neat and orderly mind and could set down those scraps in such a way that should they ever be needed they were easily found—found, that was, by anyone who had genuine need of them. Cecil himself, in fact.

And when Munck brought him the books marked with the letter 'W', Cecil could be quite sure that every scrap of information he could possibly need would have been faithfully recorded. Had it not been, then he would know it was of such little importance that it did not matter.

"Woodhall. Cedric Woodhall," he muttered as he turned the pages of closely-written facts and figures.

"If you've done aught wrong, my fine friend, 'twill all be writ here!"

It did not surprise him that alongside the name, when he found it, there was little information at all; merely the words, *See Wakeman, Christopher.*

"Cedric Woodhall—Christopher Wakeman? Both of a like initial," Cecil's agile mind supplied. "The same man . . . ?"

Eagerly he turned back the pages, his fatigue gone, for he was going to unearth something important, he knew it. Drooling with delight, he began to read.

The cocks were crowing when he blew out the candles. He was tired but triumphant, for discovering that Master Woodhall was Christopher Wakeman had been no great surprise.

What had delighted him was the fact that that particular scrap of information had been supplied, many years ago, by John Weaver, of Aldbridge.

Sir John Weaver had advised Walsingham that Wakeman was running with the hare and hunting with the hounds; that Wakeman aided Papists whilst in the service of the Crown. That made Wakeman—Woodhall—call him what you would —an accused traitor who had fled England about the time of the Armada.

Now the traitor was back and associating with Percy. It was an interesting discovery, Cecil conceded. But he was mystified too, for Harry Weaver, who had recently been mentioned to his discredit in Beelzebub's report from Ripon, was John Weaver's son and Sir John had always been loyal to the Crown and the English Church.

Surely Harry Weaver had not taken the faith of Rome?

But if not, why should he set Pursuivants to rout, then meet up with two known Papists?

Cecil flicked over the page, grateful to the long-dead Walsingham for the mine of information he had left behind him.

He read painstakingly on, then his eyes opened wide and he looked over the top of his spectacles to make sure he had seen aright.

Weaver, Harry, he read incredulously, *heir to the manor of Aldbridge. Natural son of Meg Weaver and Christopher Wakeman. Married in the church of St. Olave, Aldbridge, to Elizabeth Mary, daughter of Jane and Cedric Woodhall of York. A.D. 1588.*

Cecil swallowed hard. Harry Weaver, it seemed, was Christopher Wakeman's bastard and because of this, Elizabeth Tudor had given, for some reason, the Wakeman lands to John Weaver.

For for what reason he would have to delve deeper, but it seemed incredible that no one had noticed that Christopher Wakeman was also Cedric Woodhall and that Woodhall's daughter had married—nay, it surely couldn't be?

Robert Cecil snapped shut the heavy book. He was right for all that and it would not make for pretty telling.

Harry Weaver was not only suspected of Romanism—he was also guilty of another crime. He had wedded and bedded his natural sister, and incest was the foulest of sins!

The matter of Thomas Percy and the potman Woodhall paled into insignificance, for Robert Cecil had unearthed something far more formidable.

True, he could not use it yet, but some time soon he would summon Harry Weaver to London, for there was nothing he knew that would buy a man's loyalty so quickly and so completely as the threat of denouncement. A man who has wed his sister and fathered bairns on her, like as not will do much to keep his guilt quiet.

Cecil's smile oozed contentment. He rubbed his eyes—just

one thing more to be done and then he could go to bed and sleep like a baby.

A letter to his man in Ripon; instructions to Beelzebub, the ugly one, to watch Master Harry Weaver diligently and to report his every movement.

Bit by bit, the pieces were beginning to fit together. Soon he would be able to discredit the Romanists and their accursed Jesuit shepherds and set England free of their like for all time.

Soon, Cecil gloated, he would have his scapegoat to present to King James, then all would at last be well.

He smiled and took up his pen.

CHAPTER SEVEN

1605

THOMAS PERCY's new servant looked at his homespun smock and quirked his mouth into a grin. He must, he thought, find another inn from which to buy the ale, for the jug he carried had already been filled and emptied twice that morning. Soon the innkeeper would remark upon the vast quantities his master appeared to drink and it wouldn't do to attract even the slightest attention to the new tenant at Whinniard's.

But digging a tunnel through the foundations built to endure until the crack of doom was hard work, especially for gentlemen whose experience of spade-work amounted to little more than the gentle planting of a rosebush.

It was a pity that he couldn't lend a hand now and again, but someone must keep watch whilst the digging was being done and who better than Master Percy's manservant?

Lovingly he patted the tinderbox in his jerkin. His time would come when the hard labour was over and he would be required to lay the powder trail, light the slow-match . . .

Carefully, he bolted the door that opened onto the street. It had become second nature to him to secure the doors before he walked down the slimy steps that led to the cellars. Not that he had so far found cause to be so cautious, but Master Percy's servant was not given to taking undue risks.

Slowly he negotiated the steps, candle held high. They would be glad of a draught of cool ale, those men who worked so hard in the heat of early summer. He could have felt sorry for them had they shown the slightest signs of feeling sorry for themselves. But despite the enormity of their task, they were in good heart, even though they had occasionally expressed a doubt that the tunnel would ever be finished on time.

The sight of the ale-jug brought a smile to the begrimed faces of the men who slowly emerged from the dark of the tunnel-mouth, rubbing their backs and flexing their arms, glad to be able to stand upright once more.

"By Our Lady, Guy, that ale is a fine sight," Thomas Winter grinned.

"An' you'll not get a drop if you don't use my new name. You must forget Guy Fawkes. I am John Johnson, servant to Master Percy and caretaker of his London house. How will I ever learn to be Johnson if my friends conspire to make me forget him?" he laughed.

Carefully he filled drinking horns.

"How is the digging?" he asked.

"Not well," John Wright retorted sourly. "It's like digging through a castle keep."

"He's right," Percy confirmed sombrely. "At this rate we shall never be done in time. We must have help."

"Then let me take my quarter," Fawkes offered.

"No, Guy. You are the only one of us who dare be seen in this house, for you are the only one of us—apart from me —who has any business here. We need you to keep watch."

"Then who . . . ?"

"We must have more like ourselves—men we can trust," Catesby pondered.

"Then who more trustworthy than our own kin?"

Winter refilled his horn.

"I'd wager they already scent that something is in the wind. Why don't we sound them out?"

"Who had you in mind, Tom?"

"My brother Robert, for one. Rob would gladly help, I

know it. And there's my sister Dorothy's husband. By Jesu, I'd like a florin for every time I've seen him crack the head of a Pursuivant! John Grant would help us!"

"Aye, and I've got a brother with a strong arm," John Wright volunteered eagerly. "Young Christopher would come in with us."

"There's Bates, too," pondered Catesby. "He's a good Romanist and though he never questions my comings and going, he must know something is afoot. Maybe it would be as well if Bates were brought in."

"Master Catesby," Fawkes ventured hesitantly, "I mind the need for more diggers, but what will become of the Lambeth house where we are to store the powder? It's a lonely enough place, but it is often left empty and there'd be nothing to stop a vagrant from sheltering there—maybe even trying to light a fire—"

"You're right, Guy," Catesby acknowledged, "and I think I know of yet another who would help. Dear God, if we did but know it, the streets of London are thick with men who would throw their lot in with ours."

"But is this man trustworthy, Robert?"

"Yes, I'd trust him. He's a Derbyshire man and a devout Romanist. I reckon Master Keyes would do nicely to take care of the Lambeth house."

"Then the sooner we find these willing men, the better I'll be pleased," John Wright grinned, spitting on his blistered palms. "I swear I've never worked so hard before!"

"Then what say you?"

Thomas Percy set down his drinking horn. "I agree with you; we must find more men of trust and find them quick or we'll never have the digging finished."

Purposefully he picked up his shovel, then froze.

At first he thought it had been a trick of his ears or of the wind, maybe, that blew up-river and bore the sound in some uncanny way into the cellar.

But the wind cannot take the tolling of a bell and thrust it into the bowels of the earth so that the solemn pealing fills the air around a man and shakes the earth beneath his feet. It cannot take a sound and magnify it so that it crashes into a man's head and obliterates all thought.

"Do you hear it?" he croaked, "or has the devil got my reason?"

He had no need to ask. The faces of those about him were set into white masks in which terror-stricken eyes shifted from side to side.

They all heard the awful tolling that filled the cellar and vibrated from the walls and the stone arches of the roof above them. And as with Percy, it wrapped them round and possessed them so that they wanted to struggle against it and break its spell.

Fawkes was the first to move, willing his body into flight, taking the steps two at a time, fear urging his feet into super-human effort. Desperately he shoved at the trap-door above his head and sent it clattering back against the stone floor of the kitchen. He heaved himself from the dark cavity and stood trembling in the sane, familiar room, every nerve-end tingling with stark terror. With a conscious effort he gulped air into his lungs then noisily exhaled it, willing himself into calmness.

Then the sound was suddenly gone, releasing him, giving back his sanity.

Slowly he dragged his feet to the hearth and lit a candle at the fire. Reluctantly he walked back into the cellar.

"I thought it might have been some bell that was ringing outside," he said lamely. "Did we imagine it, do you think?"

The candle flame made shadows that rose and fell against the walls, for his hands still trembled.

He was amazed to find that he was holding a bottle.

It was an ordinary bottle—the kind that might be found in any house, but he had grasped it without thought.

"That's what put paid to it," he gasped. "It's my holy water!"

He shook his head, bemused.

"I must have reached for it, unthinking, and the evil ceased."

He poured a little into the palm of his hand and one by one they placed a finger in it and signed themselves with the all-protecting cross.

"Jesu," whispered John Wright. "What was it, do you think? I've heard many a bell, but never one that possessed me and turned my blood to ice."

"Was it the devil?"

"Or a warning . . . ?"

"It was like the ringing of the death-bell. It could have been ringing for us!"

"Damn it, then it shall not have us!"

Fawkes jerked into action, shaking his precious water onto the floor, flicking it with his finger-tips against the walls, scattering it like divine rain into the dark corners and the gaping tunnel-mouth.

"There, it is done! Be damned, now, to the evil!"

One by one they fell to their knees, blessing themselves continuously.

"Pray for a sign," Catesby whispered. "Pray that Our Lady may succour us and protect us."

They knelt there for a long time, then returned to their digging, but their hearts were sad and they were afraid.

*   *   *

Harry Weaver smiled indulgently at his wife who sat opposite him, stitching a shirt of fine silk. He would never tire of her, he thought. Each time he looked at her, she grew a little more beautiful.

Their uniting had been a love-match; the son of a noble had married a clerk's daughter and it had hardly caused the tilting of an eyebrow.

Soon Margaret and Diccon, their first-born, would feel the pleasure and pain of first love and Harry was determined they would not be forced into marriages they were opposed to.

"My lady?" he whispered.

Beth Weaver glanced up.

"You were far away. What were you thinking about so earnestly, sweeting?"

"No, I am never far from you; it's just that I still get a strange feeling when you call me *my lady*."

A small frown creased her forehead.

"I liked being Mistress Weaver far better; but so long as I am your woman, you may call me what you wish."

"I love you, woman," Harry smiled, desiring her unashamedly with his eyes.

"Sir," Beth blushed, "I beg of you to be serious. I am worried about Margaret."

"She has offended you, my lady?"

"No, but she's been having strange fancies and now she's got Diccon as bad as herself."

"Diccon is too easy-going," pronounced Harry, smiling fondly, for all that. "But tell me, what has young Meg been up to?"

"She has not been disobedient, but she insists she is for ever seeing a man who's ugly as sin sneakng into bushes or idling by the gates."

"A beggar . . . ?"

"I don't know. She took him to be that, at first. She first noticed him about a week ago when he came for food from the dole-cupboard."

"And he's been skulking around ever since? You know, Beth," Harry Weaver tried to settle his face into a look of displeasure, "the food in your dole-cupboard is too good and too plentiful. It's a wonder we don't get half the beggars in the Riding sneaking in and out of bushes or making their home at our gates!"

"But we have so much, Harry, and I have not forgotten what it is to be hungry . . ."

Harry walked over to where his wife sat and laid his finger gently on her lips.

"That was a long time ago, my lady. You will never want again . . ."

He kissed the tip of her nose, closing his eyes so that he might not see the love that shone in her face.

"Now, tell me of Mistress Margaret's man of mystery and I'll look out for him. Ugly as sin?" he grinned. "He'll be easy enough recognised."

"She said his nose is deformed and he has a long scar beneath his right eye. And his left ear looks as if a hungry wolf had taken a bite at it."

"Or the sword of justice partly severed it!"

In many parts, rough justice was still administered and the splitting of his nose or the removal of an ear could have been the price paid by a convicted thief.

Then he shrugged his shoulders. A man so branded would never be able to find work; more than likely the creature imagined he'd found himself a soft billet and intended to stay as long as he could near the Weaver's bounteous dole-cupboard.

But for all that, Harry decided, it might be best to move the man on, for it could be he was a bad lot.

"Tell our eldest daughter to stop hunting for felons who hide in bushes," Harry grinned, "and tell her it might be commendable if she were to sit with her grand-dam a bit more, and read to her!"

"I will, husband," Beth promised gravely.

"And as for Diccon—he'll be back to York and his schooling again, so he'll be out of mischief. It's different now," he grumbled in the way of every father, "in my school-days, there weren't so many holidays! We had to work hard!"

"My, but it must have been hard work, all that wenching!"

Twin dimples of mischief flickered in Beth's cheeks.

"Hussy!" he laughed, pulling her into his arms. "You should be glad I spent so much time courting you. My Latin may not be as good as it might, but god-damn it, I'm a magnificent lover!"

He reached out for her and Beth's body tingled at his touch.

Dear God, she thought, I am so happy, it is sinful. Forgive me such happiness, but let me keep it, for all that?

Agnes Muff walked into the room without ceremony. She stood for a moment, unheeding, for love was so abundant in the home of the Weavers and no one minded being seen demonstrating it.

"There's a stranger to see you, Sir Harry. He won't give his name for he says you'll not know it. Will I let him in?"

Harry sighed, then he grinned.

"Aye, Agnes."

Reluctantly he freed Beth from his arms.

"Do you think," she asked gravely, "that he could be the mystery man?"

But when the stranger stood diffidently in the doorway, they knew he was not.

"Sir," he faltered. "I am grateful to you for seeing me. I have come to thank you."

A smile touched his thin, gentle face and he pushed wispy hair from his forehead with a nervous, jerky gesture.

"You do not know me, Sir Harry, for when you helped my wife, I was locked away in Clifford's Tower. I am the man," he explained quietly, "whose wife and daughter you saved from the Pursuivants. And you gave money to my wife that she might pay our Recusancy fines and obtain my release."

Harry gave a nod of remembrance.

"A week gone, sir, I was set free and I wanted to thank you."

A small pain stabbed Harry Weaver's heart. It had happened the day on which his father died, over a year ago.

"An' they took their time letting you out! But I am right glad you're a free man again, master."

He held out his hand.

"Might I know your name?"

"It is Peter Fletcher, sir, and I thank you with all my heart for what you did."

"I do not need your thanks; I did what was my duty, friend. I cannot see women and children persecuted."

"But you need not have helped them. I know you are not of the faith of Rome. No man is duty-bound to aid a Papist, especially a man of the Anglican persuasion."

Harry Weaver was embarrassed. He had thought nothing of what he had done—indeed, he'd enjoyed kicking the loathsome creatures' backsides out of the house and up the street.

He said, "Think no more of it, Master Fletcher, and tell me how I can help you further."

"Nay, sir, I did not come to ask a favour of you, only to thank you for my release from prison and to tell you I shall pray for you and your family always."

"Then you have walked from Ripon—and will need to walk all the way back—just to thank me for something I had almost forgotten?"

"Aye, gladly, had it been twice as far."

"Then at least stay and eat," Beth insisted.

"I would be proud to accept your hospitality, my lady, but I will not. The sooner I am gone from your home, the better, for it would not set well for a known Romanist to be seen over long at your house."

The gentle little man hesitated, stunned into silence by the look of thunderous anger that leapt to Harry Weaver's face.

"Never fear, sir," Fletcher hastened. "I came privily and carefully. None saw me come and none shall see me when I leave."

"Damn it man," Harry Weaver roared, his temper in full spate, "I'll not be told who shall and shall not visit my house! By the death, you talk as if you'd got the pox on you! To the devil go your protests, master. You'll away to the kitchens and Agnes Muff shall give you victuals. I'll be cursed if you'll leave my home without taking my hospitality!"

Beth smiled and motioned to Fletcher to follow her. She had not been told about the incident, but doubtless it had slipped her husband's mind in the misery of his homecoming. It was, she thought proudly, exactly the kind of thing he would do. Probably, she supposed, it was due to his red hair; such people were often possessed of a quick temper; Master Woodhall, her mother's husband, had had one.

It was strange, she thought, that both he and Harry should have the same unusual colouring; stranger still that the one she had feared and the other she loved to distraction. The man she once believed to be her father had long ago vanished and the memory of him was hazy, but sometimes, when she was so happy that her body ached, she thought of Cedric Woodhall and shivered.

She forced her thoughts to those less fortunate than herself.

"Come, Master Fletcher," she smiled at the little man, "and I will find food for you."

*   *   *

Robert Cecil sighed and looked with dismay at the pile of documents and letters the King's Messenger had carried from York.

Not so long ago, he had written to the Council demanding they bestir themselves and be more mindful of the keeping of King James's northern kingdom.

They had not only awakened from their slumbers, it seemed, but must now be nursing their aching hands if the pile of letters on his table was anything to go by.

Carefully he broke the seals, glancing through them so that they might be placed in some order of importance.

His eyes lighted on a cyphered signature. His man in the North Riding was an atrocious writer and were he not so useful and his reports so reliable, it might have been a good idea to have had him schooled in penmanship.

But despite their lack of scholarship, one letter from Beelzebub, thought Cecil, was worth an epistle of the worthless froth he seemed doomed to read endlessly.

He smiled to note a snippet of gossip here, a breath of scandal there. Such gems could be stored for future use. Old indiscretions could be made to rattle like a skeleton in an empty closet and yield rich dividends if properly manipulated.

Cecil's eyes opened wider, surprised to read that Sir John Weaver had died of the Black Death a twelve-month past and now his son had assumed the title of the manor of Aldbridge. So much the better, Cecil mused. Regretful as it was that the Crown should lose so loyal a servant as John Weaver, his death was not without its compensations.

Now Harry Weaver had more to lose; would be more amenable than ever to a nod of warning.

And it seemed to Robert Cecil as he patiently unravelled Beelzebub's childish mass of scrawl, that Sir Harry Weaver was sailing too close to the wind for his own good and needed more than a nod. Now, it seemed, he was receiving visits from known Romanists.

By the death, it hadn't taken the man Fletcher long to make contact with his protector. One week out of prison and he was at Harry Weaver's home and remained there, seemingly, from mid-afternoon until near sunset.

The King's secretary drummed his fingers on the table. He had been right to pay heed to his instinct. Something was afoot in the north and it could be linked to Tom Percy and his mysterious comings and goings in London. It was fairly certain that Harry Weaver was Christopher Wakeman's bastard and that Wakeman, under another name, had been inveigled into the Tower arsenal.

Now Percy had taken the lease of Whinniard's tenement that butted onto Parliament House and had installed a servant there; a surly fellow, by all accounts, who refused to be drawn into conversation, going about his business with downcast eyes.

And a strange assortment of men had started to visit Whinniards; Robert Catesby, avowed Papist; Thomas Winter, a gentleman in Mounteagle's service; and John Wright of Ploughlands, whose brother had been seen in Harry Weaver's company.

Somewhere was a key to the mystery, Cecil fretted, but one thing was certain. James Stuart's absence in the hunting field would mean that he would be left in peace for several days and it would allow him a little time for his own thoughts; thoughts about Lord Mounteagle, for instance, the man who employed Thomas Winter.

Mounteagle owed him a favour, thought Cecil complacently, for who but himself had been instrumental in the restoration of Mounteagle's estates and title? He had been grateful for help received, embracing the English Church to confirm where his future loyalties lay.

Now Mounteagle was one of Cecil's tame pigeons, a willing decoy for the wild ones yet unbelievably still trusted by Romanists.

Mounteagle seemed to have acquired the knack of pleasing both sides, a fact that suited Robert Cecil well.

Nevertheless, thought Cecil testily, he had not yet been able to find the purpose of the secret visits to Whinniard's tenement nor was Percy, according to information received, making use of the man he had helped to place in the Tower arsenal.

Reports stated that the red-headed potman was a quiet and orderly fellow, doing his work with care and enthusiasm and keeping his hands in his pockets, for none of the King's gunpowder appeared to be missing.

But Cecil's trusted instinct buzzed like a bee inside his head. He must be patient and tread softly, taking care not to alert the men at Whinniard's or set them on their guard in any way.

Sooner or later, one of them would make a false move. He would give them all the rope they needed, thought Cecil, it didn't matter. Before long, he'd have them all dancing on the end of it!

CHAPTER EIGHT

IT WAS June, full-blown and sweltering, and the streets of London stank in the heat of the afternoon sun. Slowly the man in the smock of a servant approached the pile of coal that blocked the narrow alley.

He walked with care, for although most men would offer no more than a passing glance at the emptying of a coal-cellar, to those who dug like moles in the gut of the earth, the simple action could well have had a sinister purpose.

The men in Whinniard's tenement had heard the noise as they laboured, a peculiar rushing, slithering sound directly above their heads, and it chilled their bones into immobility.

"We must be below the storerooms of Parliament House."

"The coal-store, like as not."

". . . and they are shifting coal."

"Have they heard the noise of our digging?"

They stood now in the cellar at Whinniard's, cold with fear, despondent and apprehensive.

"I say we make a run for it!"

"Nay, be still and wait it out."

"For all that, I'd liefer know what's going on . . ."

"I will go upstairs and see what's afoot," Guy Fawkes volunteered. "There's no one will pay much heed to me."

"Then have a care, Guy."

"The street could be full of Pursuivants."

"Or Cecil's troopers!"

So he'd promised them he would be careful. No one

bothered over much about a servant. Like as not, they wouldn't even give him a second glance.

But for all his outward show of bravery, Fawkes felt his heart thumping as he neared the heap of coal.

He stood for a time watching the man at his shovelling, glancing around him for signs of Cecil's men.

"It's a hot day for such dirty work," he ventured eventually. "Better to have waited until the cool of evening. Shall I give you a hand, friend?"

"No, I thank you. And you are right; it would have been shifted in half the time could she only have waited. But that's women for you. *Do it this instant!*"

"Aye?" Fawkes queried, feeling a little less apprehensive.

"Aye! I tell you, that Master Bright is getting a right handful. He's wedding the widow Skinner tomorrow and nothing will do but that she moves her coal into his cellars before the ceremony!"

"This is Mistress Skinner's coal, then? It's a rare stock for a widow-woman."

"She's a coal-seller and the store is all but full. There's not so much of a sale for it when the weather's hot."

"So she's giving up her coal business?"

"No, she's taking her stock with her to her new husband's home—clearing the place out. You can't blame the woman, for she pays all of four pounds a year to rent it. It's a terrible lot for a storeroom, but maybe it's on account of it being part of the Parliament buildings."

Fawkes's heart tripped a somersault. If only they could get the empty cellar. He swallowed hard. Nay, damn it—even the devil couldn't be that lucky.

"Has the cellar been let again, do you know?" he asked, casually as he could.

"I doubt it."

The man spat on his hands and prepared to resume his shovelling.

"Four pounds—in advance—is over much to ask for a coal-hole, I reckon. You'd not catch me giving it."

Guy Fawkes closed his eyes, willing his thanks to the Almighty for such providence.

Think of it : a cellar, the far end of which must surely lie directly below the main chamber of Parliament House, and theirs for the asking, it seemed.

He wanted to run back to Whinniard's. He wanted to jump and shout for joy, for the digging had not been progressing as it should, despite the extra help they had sworn in.

He almost forgot to bolt the door of the houseplace behind him, so urgently wonderful was his news.

Pale faces turned up to greet him as he slowly negotiated the cellar steps, the light of his candle illuminating their fear.

"What is it ?"

"Are we discovered ?"

For a moment Fawkes did not speak, his eyes darting mischievously from one face to the other. Then he gave a shout of laughter and the atmosphere in the cold cellar became suddenly less tense.

"Is all well, then ? We are safe ?"

"Safe, Tom Percy ? By God, we are not only safe, but we are well-blessed ! They are shifting coal and cleaning out the store. Yon' cellar is empty and as far as I can see, there's none want to rent it, either."

And breathlessly he told them what had happened in the street above them and what he had learned from the coalheaver.

"Just when we were thinking the digging would never be done in time, this plum is dropped in our laps."

"And if we could get it, there'd be an end to our labours !"

"It will be dry, too, for the storing of the powder. The powder will have to be shifted from Lambeth—we'd agreed upon that."

"*Could* we hide the powder in the coal-hole?"

"I reckon we could—if we were careful and covered it well."

"Then pray to God," Percy remarked, "that we may be allowed to rent the widow Skinner's cellar."

"You'll try to get it, Tom?"

"By Jesu, I will. None would think twice about it if I told them I wanted to stock up coal and wood for the winter when my wife will be joining me in London."

"But wouldn't it cause suspicion—taking another cellar when you've got one already—beneath Whinniard's?"

"Why should it?" Percy demanded, confidently. "All they'll care about is getting the money. I'll offer them a year's rent. There's nothing speaks so loud in a man's favour as the jingling of sovereigns."

"And you'd move the powder from Lambeth and store it in the new place?" Fawkes insisted, relieved that his precious barrels might soon be moved from the damp house on the other side of the Thames.

"I would, an' all. There's already close on thirty barrels there. We only need a little more now. By God's Mother, if they're as lackadaisical on the day the King opens Parliament as they are in the Tower arsenal, our enemies are as good as dead already!"

Thomas Percy was right, Fawkes reasoned. They had had the devil's luck in obtaining the powder. The head storeman had scarcely glanced at their notes of authority, had scorned to count the barrels the potman passed to them. It had been so easy; at times he had scarcely been able to believe their good fortune.

"If we got the coal-hole, what would become of our digging?" John Wright asked, ever practical. "We couldn't leave a great yawning gap for any inquisitive trooper to discover."

"If—*when*—we get the coal-store, it will be a simple task to brick up the entrance to our tunnel and lime-wash it over. It would be hardly noticed then in the gloom of the cellar," Catesby retorted, confidently. "I tell you, God is on our side. Our troubles were sent to test our faith and our faith has been rewarded."

"And you really believe it?"

"I know it!" Percy exulted. "I tell you we are home and dry now!"

They sighed with reluctant relief and shook their heads in amazement, for the sudden change in their fortunes seemed too uncanny to be believed.

It was too good to be true, almost. So they laughed a little and shook their heads again as if asking silently, "Then if it is true, what is there left to do now but wait?"

But they didn't ask it and they didn't speak, for suddenly there seemed little left to say.

*   *   *

Cedric Woodhall turned his back on the massive square keep of the Tower, glad to be away from the dark and musty cellars in which he worked and clear the stink of gunpowder from his nostrils.

He wanted to look behind him, but knew that if he did he would alert the man who followed him.

He was not sure why the porter clung to him like a shadow; he only knew that to ignore him, to pretend he did not exist even, might yet lull the fellow into carelessness.

Woodhall did not like working at the Tower. Parts of it were a prison and he had known the despair of captivity, remembered even yet the awful jangling of his keeper's keys in the Fleet prison. It had been a long time ago, but it was something he would never forget.

Nor would he ever forget how near he had been to death or how he'd diced with Walsingham.

And still he had survived. It sometimes seemed to Woodhall he might yet live to see the restoration of his estates.

He walked the length of the causeway, listening to the hollow pad of his feet on the drawbridge, nodding to the guard at the gateway of the Barbican. Then he turned his back on the grim fortress and made his way quickly into Thames Street, glad to be free again, but hungry and in need of sleep that seemed to become more elusive as the days passed.

He peered ahead of him into the gathering twilight, setting his eyes on St. Paul's, picking out the collapsed spire.

It was a sign of the times, he thought. Even St. Paul's was treated more like a market and merchants did more trade inside its walls than they did in their own shops.

He wondered if ever it would be different, but he wasn't sure of anything any more. He only knew deep inside him that something tremendous was afoot. True, he had sworn an oath of secrecy before Robert Catesby and Thomas Percy, but he couldn't be certain even now what he had sworn to. He wondered yet again if he had been wise to agree to their persuading and take the work in the Tower arsenal. He'd let go enough gunpowder to hang himself twenty times over, he thought despondently, despite the notes of authority that had seemingly covered it. He could not believe that those in charge were so lax that they had not seen the glaring deficits in the powder stocks. They couldn't have been more careless if they had tossed him the keys and invited him to make free with whatever he should need.

It was strange, too, that the credentials of Catesby's servant,

Bates, had never been questioned or checked as he loaded cask after cask of powder onto the wherry tied up at the wharf by Traitor's Gate. Woodhall often wondered where Bates was taking it, but he had not dared to ask, for wherever he went so, too, went the porter, insisting it was his job to help with the loading.

That porter never gave a straight answer to any question that might be put to him, but gawped back with a daft look on his turnip face.

But he wasn't daft and Woodhall knew it.

If I were to turn sharp round now, he thought, that man will be there, a foolish grin on his face and slinking behind me like a whipped cur.

So Woodhall didn't turn round, but set his sights in the direction of the Strand and the *Irish Boy* where he lodged and still sometimes gave a hand in the ale-room.

He sighed, his body tense with apprehension. He had had enough of working in the Tower Arsenal, of looking over his shoulder and jumping at the sight of his own shadow, almost.

He was courting trouble and the ease with which he seemed to be getting away with it caused him to worry. Tomorrow, he decided, when he received his pay for the month, he would have to think very seriously about leaving London.

He had always lived a dangerous life, but he had so far survived because of his uncanny sense of self-preservation. That sense had been to the forefront of his mind lately; he could almost smell the danger all around him. Why, then, should he not leave London? Percy had enough gunpowder now to blow half the city into kingdom come if that was what he had in mind, so why not make a run for it whilst the going was good?

Wouldn't it be sensible to pocket what was due to him and head north? A man could lose himself up there for as long as he chose if he had friends to help him. And who better for that, he reasoned, than his own daughter?

Beth would be a grown woman now and long since wedded like as not, but she'd be glad to see her father again. She would keep his secret and shelter him if he needed it, of that he was sure.

And what, he wondered for the first time in many years, had become of the bitch that was his wife? Jane would be getting on in years now, maybe even dead, he thought. He wouldn't mourn her if she was. He had never loved her. He'd only married her to stop her from betraying him. But he wanted to see his daughter again. He had been fond of his beautiful little Beth.

Plans made, Woodhall's spirits lifted a little and his step became the lighter because of it.

He would enjoy seeing familiar places and faces again. He would take a look at his old home. There would be few there who would recognise him now, for John Weaver and his wife must surely be long ago dead? He wondered if Meg Weaver's brat had managed to survive into manhood and what he had made of himself.

It was strange, Woodhall thought, and diabolically unfair that the bastard he had fathered could now be living fat on what should have been *his*! But before long things might well be different, he reasoned. With James Stuart dead, there would be justice again in England. Men would be made to give back all that to which they had no right and those who had been robbed of their inheritance would receive recompense.

He threw back his shoulders and lifted his head and fancied he could smell the wide sweet acres of York county and the sight of Aldbridge, his lost inheritance, seemed to be just around the next street-corner.

Impatiently, as if eager to be away, he broke into a run.

*   *   *

"Glory be!" exulted Robert Cecil as he laid down the letter he had been reading. At last it appeared that things were beginning to move; when he'd almost been on the point of giving up and starting out on a fresh tack, the powder was at last beginning to move from the Tower arsenal.

Now, under various pretexts, Thomas Percy was presenting demands for gunpowder.

It is my duty to acquaint you, ran Carew's letter, *that close on thirty barrels have been taken, and for the life of me I cannot imagine why any man should want so much . . .*

Carew was becoming agitated and apprehensive that so much gunpowder should be falling into seemingly wrong hands.

Some men, Cecil decided, were afraid of their own shadow. Where would *he* have been now if he had given way to panic at the least sign of trouble?

He had learned to school his nerves into threads of steel, to watch and wait and play cat and mouse with cold detachment.

His man in the Tower who worked as a porter had also sent in a report which verified all Lord Carew had written. And the report had gone further, declaring that the powder was loaded onto a boat, three casks at a time, and rowed to the other side of the Thames.

Soon, thought Cecil, he would know exactly where it was going. Sufficient be it that at least there was the distance of the river between him and any chance explosion, and for that the King's secretary was grateful.

But to what use, he fretted, was the powder being put?

Were the Romanists massing? Did they hope by some show of force to try to persuade the King to grant them freedom of worship?

By Old Harry, he thought, they were an arrogant bunch. And who exactly were *they*?

Thomas Percy, who outwardly conformed and was secretly a Papist; John Wright, zealous Romanist; a man called Fawkes, about whom little was known; and Thomas Winter, a gentleman in Lord Mounteagle's service.

Now it would appear that Harry Weaver of Aldbridge was somehow entangled in the goings-on and there was the man Woodhall whom Percy had inveigled into the Tower and whose real name was Wakeman, a once-denounced traitor. Could that man be the link?

And what of Percy's servant, the man with the auburn beard and the surly face or the short, fair-haired man who tied up his boat at Tower wharf then calmly rowed gunpowder into the teeming river as cheeky as a London sparrow? Where did they all fit in?

It was like making up a picture with interlocking pieces, thought Cecil; lose a piece or two and the picture was vague and spoiled.

That a picture existed was beyond doubt and it was beginning to take shape; yet still it wasn't clear because too many pieces were missing.

But things might become a little clearer when it was known where the gunpowder was being taken. Things would be a lot clearer if he knew exactly what went on inside Whinniard's tenement. Thomas Percy had been seen there and his servant too, but there was nothing untoward in that; Percy now rented Whinniard's.

But other men had been seen entering the house and leaving it again, considerably less clean in their dress.

What were they doing—or making—there? Why should

Thomas Percy have gone to so much trouble to acquire Whinniard's when he had a perfectly adequate house over the river, at Lambeth?

At Lambeth!

Cecil smote the desk at which he sat with the flat of his hand and almost whooped for joy.

Idiot that he was for not remembering!

Percy's house, lonely and aloof on Lambeth marshes, close by a little channel that was fed by the river—a perfect place in which to secrete illicit gunpowder. He'd lay anyone a groat to an angel he was right!

Cecil reached for his bell, then impatiently strode across the room, wrenching open the door of the small private office, unable to wait for Munck to answer his summons.

"I want you to arrange for men to keep watch on Master Percy's house at Lambeth. Tell them to pay special attention to the race at the side of the house and any small boat entering or leaving it."

He rubbed his hands together in a strangely satisfied way. Given luck, there would soon be another piece to fit into his picture puzzle.

But Munck looked perplexed.

"I will do as you say at once, my lord, but your mention of Master Percy has set me to thinking . . ."

"Indeed, good Levinus?"

His clerk was becoming very adept at thinking, Cecil decided with satisfaction. He was learning fast now and learning well.

"Aye, sir. Only this morning I heard mention of Tom Percy's name in the Estates Office—I happened to have business in there—and it seems that the gentleman had just left. He was making enquiries, I understand, about Mistress Skinner's coal-store."

"A coal-store? What in heaven's name does he want a coal-store for?"

"It set me wondering, too. 'Master Percy,' I said to myself, 'has a good house in Lambeth, but needs must be nearer Court, so he leases Whinniard's. Now he wants to be nearer still'. . ."

"Nearer to Court? What do you mean, man? Where is this coal-store?"

"Why, my lord, it's beneath the Lords' Chamber at Parliament House."

"*Beneath* Parliament House, you say?"

"Just so, and hence my little joke about his being even nearer to Court, although why Master Percy should want another cellar when there's a good one at Whinniard's is beyond me."

Another cellar? Cecil's brain whirred into action.

What was Percy up to? Why had he wanted Whinniard's and why now did he want the cellar beneath the House of Lords?

And what was Percy doing with all the gunpowder he had acquired? Surely he didn't want to store the stuff in Mistress Skinner's coal-hole? By God, he thought, it would be a mite dangerous if he did. One careless spark from a spur or a boot-iron and the lot would go sky-high and everybody else for miles around, an' all!

He stopped. There was an itching in his nose and his teeth had started to water.

"God's death," he jerked incredulously. It couldn't be. *It simply couldn't be!*

Robert Cecil felt a tingling at the nape of his neck and it iced its way to the tips of his toes.

He ran his tongue round his suddenly dry lips and whispered, "Do you know why Thomas Percy wants gunpowder,

Master Munck? And do you know why he wants Mistress Skinner's coal-cellar?"

The clerk shook his head, unspeaking.

"Then I'll tell you and listen to me good, for I'll not say it twice."

He shook his head, bemused, reluctant almost to say it at all.

"They are going to kill the King."

He spoke slowly and quietly, emphasising each word as though all the while debating with himself.

"They are going to pack explosives beneath the Lord's chamber and send all in it to kingdom come. I'd wager all I've got on it," he whispered, wonderingly, "all I've got!"

Cecil's heart thumped madly and he was afraid and elated at one and the same time.

And they were planning their evil for the opening of Parliament, a time when most men who were hostile to their cause would be gathered together! It was a clever and daring plot.

But he, Cecil decided, was cunning too. If they thought to get the better of him, then they were fools.

He shook his head, aware that Munck was silently watching him.

"Well, man, what ails your feet?" he snapped. "Away and see to it that Master Percy's house is watched—the *Lambeth* house, I mean!"

He shuffled to the outer door.

"And not a word to a soul about what has passed between us, mind! If you so much as breathe one word of it, I'll have your tongue on a platter!"

Cecil hesitated, his hand on the door-sneck.

"Who have we in Mounteagle's household? Is it Ward?"

"Aye, my lord—Thomas Ward."

"And he's trustworthy, eh?"

"He is; he misses nothing and his reports are regular and prompt."

Cecil nodded absently and closed the door of his room behind him, locking it carefully, making for the far end of the building where the Administrators and their scriveners worked.

Perhaps a visit to the Estates Office to make sure that all were working diligently; to make doubly sure whilst he was about it that Thomas Percy was given the lease of Ellen Skinner's coal-cellar.

Percy and his unknowns seemed hell-bent on destruction. He must give them every possible encouragement, Cecil mused, to destroy *themselves*!

CHAPTER NINE

THE man with the red hair walked jauntily, the early morning air cold in his nostrils. There was excitement inside him, for the last time he travelled the Aldbridge road had been in the darkness with John Weaver's words ringing in his ears.

"You have six days to leave these shores . . ."

When a man is branded traitor, he has little choice but exile and the years he spent in France seemed to stretch into a lifespan.

Now he travelled light, tramping the road with the bite of autumn on the land, glad to leave the stench of London behind him.

On either side, the fields had been ploughed and lay in long straight furrows, awaiting the winter frosts, and here and there in cottage gardens apples still hung ripening.

The summer had been good and even yet the weather was gentle with milch-cows still grazing the rich grass and swine running free in the autumn-tinted woodlands, grubbing for roots and acorns, growing steadily fatter for winter killing.

He had never appreciated the bounty of his youth, Wood-hall mused, but it had seemed then that the riches to which he had been born would last for ever.

He shrugged, eager to miss nothing of the once-familiar countryside, thinking about London, wondering if his sudden flight from the Tower arsenal had caused comment.

He had taken his time in journeying north, working if the chance presented itself and managing to live well enough.

He had been on the road for almost three months, but it was not unpleasant, for he had travelled the last hundred miles in the safety of a pack-horse train. A lonely traveller could do worse than attach himself to a carrier, for the men who tended the horses were seasoned travellers and knew every mile of the way.

And so he journey into Yorkshire in the company of Mr Pickford's thirty horses, their bells jingling to warn off the devil, for horses were especially prone to the evil eye.

Then in early October he sighted the comforting walls of York and it was as if he had never been away. Nothing had changed. The horse-fair was in full sway as it had always been in the days after Michaelmas; the King's Manor where he once worked, and the little huddle of houses in the Minster Yard where once he had lived, still stood there, untouched by the passing of time.

It had not taken long to find the whereabouts of Jane his wife, and Beth.

"Taken terrible badly was Mistress Woodhall and near to starvation the pair of them," confirmed an old woman. "And then a young noble came and they rode off with him; 'twas the last that folks in the Yard ever saw of them. Were they kin of yours, sir?"

"No," Woodhall lied easily, "I am but making some enquiries for a friend. Tell me, what was he like, this young noble?"

"Oh, it's a long time gone; I couldn't be sure, but if I mind aright they did say the young man lived at Aldbridge, where-ever that may be."

Cedric Woodhall felt a giddy churning in his belly. Beth had ridden off with a young noble. And was that youngling a love-child, gotten at Childermas in the merriment of Christmas? Had he been fathered in a cow-shed where the air was sweet with the scent of hay?

115

Woodhall was young again at the thought of it. There was a throbbing in his loins and Meg Weaver was in his arms, her body arching itself against his.

"Damnation!" he swore, spitting viciously as if to rid himself of all memory, all desire.

And he must rid himself of all feeling if he was to make the most of Fate's bounty, for his daughter could well have married Meg Weaver's son. They could have lain together in the filth of incest and gotten bairns to cement their sin. And if they had, it was all to the good for now, whatever the outcome of the London business, he had become possessed of knowledge that would ensure his wellbeing for the rest of his life. Would not any man pay and pay again to keep so dreadful a secret hidden? He threw back his shoulders, a new lease of life within him, feeling as he neared Aldbridge like the man he had once been. Now it was Kit Wakeman who strode the road to Aldbridge, and the world was his kicking-ball again.

At the crossroads above the village he stopped and wiped the sleeve of his jacket across his forehead. The midmorning sun shone brightly, but the sweat on his brow was one of excitement.

Below him at the foot of the hill lay the village—*his* village, be the truth known—and seeing it again set his heart thumping. Slowly he made his way towards the green where the stocks stood empty beside the inn and tethered geese nibbled the short grass.

Sheltered behind the tall old beeches stood the manorhouse, the rosy-red bricks of its newer chimneys blending with the warm sandstone walls, and as he walked closer he could see the arms of the Wakemans set into the high stone arch of the gateway; it surprised him that John Weaver had not torn them down.

But the Wakemans were all gone, save for himself. They

had not been a fruitful family, he mused, at least not in wedlock. Now there was only himself who dare not own to being a Wakeman and the child of an unhappy mating; a woman named Beth. She had never known his true identity or of the proud old family to which she rightly belonged. To have told her that would have risked the tightening of the hangman's noose about his neck.

But even if he and Beth were the last of the Wakemans, at least he'd fathered bastards in plenty, although bastards didn't count; they were only the offset of a nobleman's pleasure.

He would always remember the Childermas of long ago, for all that. As much as he was able, he had loved Meg who bore his first child. A man remembered the first time, he supposed, the more so when the child of that union had usurped his father's inheritance.

Woodhall saw Beth in the distance and it did not shock him in any way. He had been looking for her and now she had come. A servant walked beside her, carrying a basket. Beth would be about her duties, he supposed, for those who lived at the manor-house must always be mindful of the needs of their tenants. In her basket would be an assortment of lotions, potions and physic—perhaps jelly and broth too, for the sick and old.

He watched her approach with a sense of detachment, taking in her beauty as a man might gaze at a picture. Her dress was simple and she wore a blue cloak. Her hair was coiled into a pearl-trimmed net from which a few stray wisps curled softly on her cheeks.

By Our Lady, but she has grown more lovely for the keeping, Woodhall thought. He touched his hat and bowed and she inclined her head towards him, her eyes smiling kindly at the stranger.

Then she had passed him, walking towards the almshouses

as though it mattered nothing that she had passed her own flesh and blood with no more than blank politeness.

He stood for a moment, savouring the certain knowledge that his natural son had indeed married his half-sister. He wondered if their mating had got children and what those children were like. Bairns of so unholy a union were damned in the very second of their conception, for it was one of the punishments for incestuous love. Like as not they'd have idiot faces and slow wit. For a fleeting moment it irked him that his progeny should be anything less than perfect, but he shrugged it away. All that mattered was that he, Cedric Woodhall, should not be the loser.

Slowly he crossed the green, following the beck that ran beside the mill.

Did Jeffrey Miller still live there? If any one person in Aldbridge were to recognise him, it would be Jeffrey Miller, Woodhall thought sourly. But that was unlikely when his own daughter had treated him as if he were no more than a passing stranger.

Stepping back into the world of his youth, he walked down the lane that led to the back of the manor-house and the stable-yard. At this time it had always been his mother's custom to open the dole-cupboard to beggars who waited by the kitchen door.

He looked about him, the familiarity of his surroundings bringing an ache of remembrance that rose to a great pain in his throat.

To his left were the stables and at the far end of the cobbled yard was the archway that led to the pig sties and cow sheds. He and Meg Weaver once ran hand-in-hand across those cobbles, their eager young feet scarcely touching the snow, laughing at their daring, flushed with desire. And as the whole of Aldbridge danced and feasted in the great hall, they two had loved and in their passion made a love-child.

Did Harry Weaver know he had been conceived in a cow-shed or did he imagine he had been gotten between the blankets of respectable wedlock?

Woodhall joined the line of beggars, turning his head from the stink of their bodies.

But those who waited at Aldbridge manor-house had been born to poverty and knew no better. He who could own to being a Wakeman would survive and come into his own again, and by divine right all that his eyes could encompass should have been his; one day it would be his again.

"We shall not have long to wait," said the one-armed beggar who stood beside Cedric Woodhall. "The Lady Elizabeth usually walks the rounds of the village before attending here. And the dole from this house is worth a wait."

"Did I perchance see the Lady Elizabeth on my way here? A handsome lady, wearing a cloak of blue velvet?"

"Aye, that would be her. She has a rare compassion. But maybe she understands poverty, for I once heard it said she was humble-born and the daughter of a scrivener. But what matter when the dole's good, eh?"

Anger stabbed at Woodhall like a red-hot knife. Humble born? By God, her blood was as good as any in the county and he wanted to stand there and proclaim it. But he put his tongue in his cheek and when she handed him cheese and bread, he blessed her as those before him had done, his eyes meeting hers as he did so.

He might have imagined the quick intake of her breath or a sudden jerking of her head, but he couldn't be sure. He tipped his hat and shuffled away through the stableyard and into the lane, his body trembling.

Beth *had* married Harry Weaver! He should be glad and when he had composed himself, he reasoned, he doubtless would be. But how strange that from the whole of Christendom *his* daughter should choose to bed with *his* bastard.

Life was changing for the better, reasoned Woodhall. He smiled, doffing his hat to the young girl who walked towards him.

"Bid you good-day, mistress," he said, easily.

The girl answered his smile.

"A blessing on you, fair miss, for your father's bounty."

He indicated the half-eaten food in his hands.

"You are Sir Harry Weaver's little maid, are you not?"

"I am Margaret Weaver, though most call me Young Meg," she replied.

Her name jolted him, for although she resembled Beth, she was more like Meg—his Meg of the heartsease.

"Margaret Weaver, is it? And why is so beautiful a maid walking alone? Where are all your swains? Don't tell me," he said with feigned surprise, "that you are destined for a convent?"

Margaret Weaver laughed. She liked this man who begged his food yet spoke to her as an equal.

"I am alone because I have no sweetheart and because Diccon, my twin, has gone back to school."

She settled herself beside him, eager to break the monotony of her day.

"I wish I'd been born a lad, an' all," she sighed. "Diccon has all the fun and I must stay at home and be schooled by my lady mother."

"Then stay and talk a while to a lonely old wanderer, Mistress Margaret. It would please him greatly if you would."

He looked at the girl who sat down beside him as though she had always known him. She had Beth's pale-gold hair—Meg's hair had been that colour, too—and Beth's clear blue eyes with mischief in them like suppressed laughter. She smiled at him and he smiled gravely back, liking her despite himself. He was glad he had been wrong and she was not moon-faced or slow-witted, for wasn't she his grand daughter, truth known? Wasn't she doubly so, if he cared to think of both sides of it?

"Tell me about yourself, Mistress Margaret," he said.

*　　*　　*

"I do declare," Anne Weaver grumbled at supper-time, "that this place is miserable as a Lenten church! Where is everybody?"

Beth Weaver raised her head.

"Harry is at the stables. His new mare is due to foal at any time and Margaret is with the children."

"In disgrace, I suppose? What has she been up to now?"

"I told her she must take her supper with the younglings tonight and then rock Anna to sleep."

"Ah." The old head nodded wisely. "And what did she do to merit her banishment from grown-up supper?"

"She was over-late for her dinner at midday, you know it, and she was late because—"

Beth shrugged and pushed away her half-eaten meal.

Anne waited, picking up a russet apple and rubbing it gently in her cupped hands. She said obliquely, "It is one of the banes of old age—not being able to eat an apple," she sighed. "When a body's teeth drop out, there's nothing left but pap."

She sighed again, sniffing the rough brown skin with yearning.

"I will skin it for you, my lady, and chop it up small."

Beth took the apple, peeling it with a concentration that defied further questioning.

"I am grateful to you, Beth, but it is not the same. To bite one's teeth into an apple, to feel the crunch and tingle of it . . ."

She picked up a spoon and deliberately dropped it with a clatter.

121

Beth looked up sharply and read the unspoken question in the old eyes. Then she said, with relief, "Yes, my lady, I am bothered."

"Aye, I know. Tell me about it."

"Margaret was late to supper because she was talking to a beggar."

"Ha! The times I've told her to keep away from beggars with their fleas and spots and scabs! Has she begged your pardon yet?"

"She has not. She said, if you please, that she was improving her education. The man spoke to her in French, she said. He was a learned man it seems, and amusing to talk to. She took to him . . ."

Beth made a small helpless gesture with her hands.

"What was he like, this educated beggar?"

Anne Weaver's nose began to twitch.

"He was elderly but his hair was red, still—"

Anne's mouth went dry. She didn't want to know any more, yet she asked the question for all that.

"And you know him?"

"Aye, madam. He was at the dole-cupboard at noon."

She reached out for the old hands that lay calmly on the table, seeking their comfort and wisdom.

"I know him and he knows me—his eyes told me so when I gave him food."

She took a deep, steadying breath.

"Margaret's beggar is Cedric Woodhall, my father!"

"Sweet Jesu, never say that, Beth! *Cedric Woodhall did not beget you*! Never forget it!"

Beth closed her eyes and Anne felt the trembling of her hands within her own.

"No . . . no. I know it, but he doesn't. He still thinks I am his, I am sure of it."

"And you are quite certain it was Woodhall? You couldn't have been mistaken?"

"Would to God I could be," she said, despairingly.

"So!" Anne Weaver's eyes took on a faraway look as they always did when she was remembering. "The traitor has returned? Come to look at what might have been his, no doubt. Likely he's been petitioning the King for the return of his estates and gotten a flea in his ear for his trouble!"

"Perhaps he has just come for charity, my lady. He is old now and maybe lonely."

"And you would give him charity, knowing what he is? Do you realise that there is still a price on his head? Woodhall or Wakeman—either way he's a proven traitor—you cannot help him. Only be thankful he is not your father and you can disown him without fear of conscience."

"You are right; you are always right, madam. I will tell my fears to Harry. He will know what is best to be done."

*   *   *

The soldier clattered thankfully into the stableyard, reined up his horse, then walked stiffly towards the knot of men gathered round the mare and her newly-dropped foal. He rubbed his buttocks with the flat of his hands and flexed the muscles of his shoulders, glad the long ride from York was at an end.

His eyes lit up as he saw the white foal.

"By Old Harry, but there's a fine little filly!"

"Aye, she's mine," Harry grinned, his face flushed with pride.

"Sir Harry Weaver?"

The rider jumped to attention, taking a parchment from his pouch, handing it over.

"Porrit, sir, of the Earl of Salisbury's troop, newly from London."

"You've ridden from London?"

"No, sir, I am posted to York, but if my luck holds good, I'll be riding back there on escort duty."

Harry Weaver puzzled over the seal on the parchment, frowning at its strangeness, for it was not the imprint of the Council of the North.

"From the Earl of Salisbury," supplied the soldier. "Robert Cecil . . ."

"By the Lord, but that man collects titles like I collect horses," Harry grinned, but wondering for all that what possible business the King's chief minister could have with a north-country squire.

The taxes were paid, the levy of men for the militia long since equipped and despatched, the manor was in good order.

The letter was short and to the point, commanding Harry Weaver of Aldbridge to attend the Earl of Salisbury at the palace of Whitehall with all due expediency.

"I am to go to London," he mused, folding the parchment carefully and pushing it into his pocket. "Damn it, and the winter coming on an' all. Have any others received such letters?"

"Not to my knowing, Sir Harry, but I did hear it said that the Archbishop of York is to journey to London in two days' time. Maybe you'll be able to travel with His Grace."

"Lord, but that will take weeks! I'd thought to make the journey alone, and quickly."

"Given the choice, I'd not go alone, sir. The days are shortening. Best to go with the Archbishop under escort. You'll fare better that way for victuals and lodgings."

Mystified and annoyed, Harry Weaver ordered that the trooper's horse be rubbed down and fed and the trooper quartered for the night in the stable-loft.

"I am summoned to Whitehall," he announced without

ceremony as he seated himself at the supper table. "I leave in the morning."

Beth's face registered alarm.

"But why such haste, Harry? What is wrong?"

"Nothing is wrong, love, and there is no real haste, save that I am to travel south with the Archbishop of York and his escort the day after tomorrow. There is no need for you to worry, Beth. I cannot possibly be in bad grace."

"Aye, Beth," soothed Anne Weaver, "cease your worrying. I mind the time my John was summoned to London—"

She sat still, staring at her hands, remembering the long hungry days she had spent with only Goody Trewitt for company and food so precious she had all but starved.

Then suddenly she smiled, remembering how she had run to welcome John home in the darkness of the early spring morning, her arms flung wide and tears of joy wet on her cheeks. He had given her a fine hat that day and laid the manor of Aldbridge at her feet.

"He came back the richer for the Queen's favour. Maybe the Stuart is going to reward you too, eh, Harry?"

"I want nothing from him, save to be left alone," he retorted sharply. "It may well be that the King may have something in mind for the northern counties—and not before time, either, for up here we might as well live in Cathay for all the notice they take of us!"

"I'd liefer be left in peace, for all that," Beth's voice trembled close to tears. "I don't want you to go, husband. I am afraid for you."

She clung to him and he felt her body shaking.

"I shall be all right, love, and I will bring you back silk and velvet."

He was beginning to warm to the adventure for he had never journeyed farther afield than Leicester. A trip to London might not be such a bad thing, and he had not yet sworn allegiance to the Stuart. It might be as well if he were to do that. He reached out and cut off a rib of beef, suddenly hungry. After all, it wasn't every day a man got a finely bred filly and a summons to Whitehall. And Jeffrey could take care of Aldbridge for him.

He smiled at Beth.

"Cheer up, my lady. They're not going to cut off my head," he grinned.

But Beth was bothered. Now she would have to deal alone with Cedric Woodhall's unwanted intrusion, for she was determined she would not burden Harry with such a worry on the eve of his departure. Their last night together should not be sullied by talk of a man she had hoped never to see again.

Their last night?

What a foolish thing to have thought. Of course it would not be the last time she would lay in Harry's arms. Their love was too strong for anything to part them—wasn't it?

She forced a tremulous smile to her lips, but her heart was heavy and she wanted to be sick.

Suddenly she knew fear. Something was afoot and Harry's summons to London had something to do with it.

"Sweet Jesus, what am I to do," she whispered inside her. "Why do I love my Harry so much . . . ?"

*   *   *

Master Munck coughed deferentially and handed the paper to his master.

"I have done a rough composition, my lord," he hesitated. "If there is anything you might wish to add or change . . . ?"

Robert Cecil, newly created Earl of Salisbury, carefully read what was written before grunting with satisfaction.

"It will do very well. Now you must make a fair copy then return it to my keeping. I will hold it safe until the time is right."

Scapegoat for a Stuart

"And when will that be, sir?"

"Soon, Master Munck; soon. Mounteagle is in Bath and Thomas Ward with him, but as soon as they return to London, Ward will be instructed to be on hand and someone shall deliver that letter. By Old Harry, but it will set the cat amongst the pigeons an' no mistake!"

Salisbury almost permitted himself a chuckle.

"We shall know then who the guilty ones are, friend Munck. We shall separate the sheep from the goats!"

He handed over several scraps of paper.

"More notes for your records. See to them when you have finished Mounteagle's letter."

The clerk scanned the papers. The Archbishop of York was journeying south, it seemed, and was nearing Derby.

And more interesting news—the potman who had fled the Tower arsenal had been last seen approaching Aldbridge, according to Beelzebub's latest despatch.

So that, reasoned Munck, was the cause of Sir Harry Weaver's summons to London. There would appear to be strange goings-on around York and Sir Harry, it seemed, must needs give an account of himself.

Munck smiled a little sadly and took up his quill, shaking his head in amazement at the stupidity of the wild northmen.

Would they never learn, he wondered?

CHAPTER TEN

"You cannot but agree with me, Sir Harry. In the light of all that has happened recently, I had no choice but to bring you to London."

"But God-damn it, Lord Salisbury—I protect a woman who is being set about by felons . . ."

"A *Papist*, sir, being shown the *error of her ways* by servants of the Crown."

"By thugs! Better men have been hanged for less! Do you know how evil these Pursuivants are; that all decent men despise them?"

"Do you rebuke me, Sir Harry?"

"No, my lord, but if the cap fits . . ."

"I do not like your tone, sir!" Cecil jumped to his feet, "and I think you do not appreciate the bother you have landed yourself in!"

He took a steadying breath, then sat down again, annoyed that he had allowed himself to be ruffled by the defiance of the great Northerner who should by rights have been whining for tolerance.

"You obstruct the King's servants in the lawful pursuance of their duties; you meet up with Papists—"

"Two old schoolfellows and accidentally met!"

"You receive a visit from Fletcher of Ripon, and him newly released from prison after *you* paid his fines."

"I gave money to his wife; she was penniless!"

"Then tell me about Christopher Wakeman?" Cecil flung.

Harry Weaver frowned annoyance.

"I know nothing about him, save that his father's lands were given to us by Queen Elizabeth and that Christopher Wakeman cheated the axeman by letting another die in his place."

"You know of this? Who told you?"

"My wife—who else? Her mother confessed it when she thought she was on her deathbed. Jane Woodhall knew that her husband spied for Walsingham, yet aided Papists at the same time."

For a time Cecil was taken aback. He had summoned this man to London that he might confront him with certain facts; facts that at the very least should have made him apprehensive. The dossier of evidence should have turned him into a very frightened man, eager to exonerate himself. But it wasn't turning out that way. Harry Weaver, it appeared, knew a great deal about the traitor who called himself Woodhall.

Yet there was still the guilt of his incest, Cecil reasoned. The trump-card still waited to be played.

"Did you know, Sir Harry, that I have reason to believe that Christopher Wakeman is playing with fire again?"

"Hell! I thought the man was dead!"

Harry Weaver felt a stab of alarm. He had hoped never to hear of him again, if only for Beth's sake.

"Well, he's alive and you'll appreciate my mistrust of your loyalty when I tell you he is now in Aldbridge."

"*In Aldbridge!*"

Harry Weaver jerked to his feet.

"Then I'll bid you good-day, my lord, for if what you say is true, I have no time to waste here on a fool's errand!"

Cecil flushed angrily.

"I do not waste my time on fools," he hissed, "and you will return to Aldbridge if and when I give you leave to do so!"

"Then you and your leave may go to hell, sir, for if that man is at Aldbridge, I fear for my wife's safety."

"Your wife—his daughter, eh?" Cecil craftily insinuated. Soon he'd get Weaver to admit it.

"Aye! No, damn it . . ."

Harry ran his fingers through his hair in a small worried gesture. He was becoming uneasy. He realised that to upset Cecil would do no good at all, for it seemed that Cecil, for some reason, seriously doubted his loyalty.

"Sir," he said, forcing his voice into calmness, "I don't know why I am here, but I ask you to tell me of what I am suspected so that I might set things to rights and be away to my home. I truly believe my Beth might be in danger."

"From Wakeman? He couldn't harm his own daughter, surely?"

Harry Weaver clenched his fists. Damn Cecil. Why did he keep on about the man's *daughter*?

"No, sir, I am sure he wouldn't, but if this man I know as Woodhall is in Aldbridge, be sure he's there to demand money or shelter. When my wife tells him she owes him nothing since she is not his daughter—"

"*Not* his daughter?" Cecil exploded, his mouth sagging disappointment. "Are you sure?"

With almost unbearable grief, he saw the big stick with which he had intended beating Harry Weaver into submission being wrenched from his hand.

"Aye, I'm sure—his wife cuckolded him. Walsingham let another die in his place. That man's name was Peter and he was a ploughman. It was Peter who fathered my wife and Woodhall never knew it. Mistress Woodhall looked upon her deception as a kind of justice for she had truly loved Peter. It was only when she wanted to cleanse her soul for death that she told Beth of her true parentage."

"I see," Cecil shrugged.

Weaver's statement sounded uncommon like the truth.

He drummed his fingertips on the table, his brain churning madly so that he might turn the situation to his advantage once more.

"That is why you must let me be away home," Harry Weaver interrupted his thoughts. "I think Woodhall is an evil man. If he finds out the truth, God knows what might happen."

The little hunchback spread his hands in a gesture of appeasement.

"I sympathise with you, Sir Harry. Indeed, it would seem that you did not know of Woodhall's movements nor had any recent dealings with him. But there are many things left unexplained. I am still not entirely convinced of your loyalty to King James."

Harry Weaver jumped to his feet, biting back his anger, clenching his teeth until his jaws hurt. Then he drew in a deep breath and held it until he felt his lungs must burst.

"By Our Lady, but you are a miserable fellow, my lord," he hissed, "and had I the sense I was born with, I'd see you are not worth the trouble of my anger. I am John Weaver's son and raised by him to be grateful to the Crown for all I own. Do you think I'd be fool enough to do anything to endanger my lands? Can you truly believe I would even want to? I was loyal to Queen Elizabeth and her church and I am willing to swear fealty to King James on my knees if that will satisfy you. Only let me be on my way home . . . ?"

Cecil's instinct had rarely played him false. Now it told him he had been wrong to mistrust Harry Weaver. Circumstances seemed capriciously to have misled him and he'd have to admit it, if only to himself.

But he was not one to let an opportunity slip by. He had bought the man to London and by the Lord he would get something out of it! Besides, the Yorkshireman had defied him and his eyes blazed scorn. The Earl of Salisbury did not allow any man such unpaid-for liberties.

"Come, Sir Harry; sit down and let us talk without all this muck-slinging. Likely there is a good explanation for my doubts."

Cecil was himself again. He smiled ingratiatingly.

"Let us get to the bottom of the matter and then you can be off home as fast as you like."

Harry Weaver lowered himself into the chair again.

"I tell you, sir, there is nothing to be bottomed, for I am the King's man. That it seemed otherwise is unfortunate, but I would do the same again, given the chance. I will not stand by whilst licensed thugs persecute defenceless women, no matter what their religion. And I tell you more; I think I know who has fed you these lies. He has been skulking around my house, begging from my dole-cupboard. Like as not he's the same brute who attacked Mistress Fletcher in Ripon."

"Oh?" Cecil nodded, not a little surprised. He had thought Beelzebub to be more discreet.

"Aye, sir, and if his evil nose is sniffing round my manor when I return, I'll have him whipped from the village, no matter *who* his master is!"

Robert Cecil finally conceded defeat. No guilty man would chance his luck as Harry Weaver was doing.

"Calm down, Sir Harry; calm down. You have a hot temper that matches your hair," he smiled. "I am told that Wakeman had hair like yours and look where it landed him!"

"Aye, and so had Peter the ploughman and he fared worse, my lord. Anyway, what's in red hair?"

"Nothing, Sir Harry; nothing at all, save that it is most unusual."

"So—I have unusual red hair that curls, like Wakeman's? Does that brand me traitor, too? Does that make me his kin and responsible for his wrong-doings?"

"Sir, I did not *say* that. You put words into my mouth. Did I say you were Wakeman's son? Did I, eh? Could it even be possible?"

Harry shook his head in bewilderment. The conversation was becoming ridiculous.

"My lord, I fear I have lost the drift of our talk. Despite the fact that all I own might one day have gone to Christopher Wakeman, I am a *Weaver*. I want no truck with a traitor."

"You are right, Sir Harry; we have got ourselves mixed. After all, there could be no question at all of your being kin to Wakeman, could there?"

Harry raised his hands in a gesture of resignation, then dropped them heavily to his sides.

"Sir, I beg you, let us start afresh, for I swear I am lost. I am summoned to London because you doubted my loyalty. I deny your suspicions and would welcome the chance to prove myself. I cannot say fairer than that."

Cecil reached for the wine bottle.

"Aye, circumstances can play a man false, I'll admit it. Pray drink with me that we may begin again as you suggested and start not as enemies but as friends."

"And then I will be free to go?"

"Free as a bird, sir."

Cecil filled the fine glass goblets to the brim.

"But might I ask a favour of you, Sir Harry, and if, to show there is no ill-will between us, you could grant it, I would be very glad."

Harry Weaver let go a sigh of relief.

"Only ask, my lord."

"Then deliver a letter for me."

"A letter? That would be no great trouble, but could not a page-boy or a messenger do it as well as I?"

"Perhaps, but this is no ordinary letter. It is of a most

133

confidential nature, concerned with the King's business, and it must never be mentioned again, once it has left your hands. Do you understand me?"

"I do, and you have my word that it will be as you ask. But the delivery of a letter seems a small test of loyalty, in my estimation."

"Nevertheless, it is all I ask of you, Sir Harry; that and your denial, should you ever be confronted with it, that you ever saw such a document."

"If you will assure me I am doing nothing to endanger the King's well-being, I will do as you ask."

Cecil smiled.

"I thank you, sir, and I promise you will be about King James's business."

"Then I am your man. Where is the letter?"

Cecil fingered his chin thoughtfully.

"Well . . . you are not deliver it yet—I am not sure when—but it will be soon . . ."

How long was *soon*, Harry thought with dismay. He wanted to be home. He had no desire to kick his heels in London when Woodhall was reputed to be in Aldbridge.

For all that, he said as evenly as he could, "Very well, Lord Salisbury. I am lodging at Master Boyle's house by the Charing Cross."

"I know, Sir Harry. I know."

Cecil rose to his feet and held out his hand, the interview at an end.

"We shall not meet again, but you will hear from me before long and then you'll be on your way north before you know it. And if you will do me one last favour, Sir Harry? Should you come across Wakeman on your manor, hand him, if you will, to the Sheriff at York, despite the bond between you."

"The *bond*? Between Wakeman and *me*?"

Damn it, what bee was buzzing in Cecil's bonnet now?

"Forgive me, Sir Harry; I was joking. But as I said, the pair of you do have the most unusual hair . . ."

Cecil was well satisfied. He had delivered his parting thrust and there was nothing more to be done. He had, he hoped, sown the seeds of doubt.

If Weaver knew of his true parentage, it was as well he should be reminded he had been fathered out of wedlock and by a traitor; if he did not, then it wouldn't hurt to give him food for thought.

With luck, Cecil reasoned, Harry Weaver might yet be persuaded into service. Men of his calibre were thin on the ground.

He bowed graciously, noting with complete pleasure the look of perplexity on the Yorkshireman's face.

"I bid you good-day then, Sir Harry, and remember—we have never met—you and I, eh?"

*   *   *

Reluctantly Beth Weaver wrenched her thoughts away from London town and picked up her sewing. The shirt she stitched was to be a homecoming gift for Harry and it was almost finished, save for the lace at the cuffs and neck.

Ann Weaver turned painfully in her chair.

"Drat that Margaret! Where is she? By the time she brings my reading glass, I'll have lost the urge to read!"

"Margaret is restless when Diccon is at school," Beth soothed. "They are twins, remember."

"Aye," Anne grumbled, "and I'll swear Goody Trewitt mixed them at birth."

"You left it in the kitchen, my lady, not in your bedchamber," the subject of Anne's affectionate criticism tossed the missing glass onto her grand-dam's lap. "And guess who is outside in the great hall? Go on—guess!"

135

Beth's sewing slid to the floor at her feet.

"Harry! Your father is back?"

"I fear not."

The man who stood in the doorway bowed, then smiled, a curious, half-remembered smile that caused Beth's hand to fly to her mouth, stifling the gasp that rose in her throat.

"He was at the kitchen door, asking to see you," Margaret Weaver explained breathlessly. "I told him to come in."

"Who is it? Who has come?" Anne peered into the gloom.

"It is my friend who speaks to me in French. He has come to see my mother."

"And thank her for the excellence of her dole," the man offered, stepping into the room.

"You asked a beggar in here, Margaret?" Anne demanded. But Beth was on her feet.

"Leave us, Margaret! Go to the younglings and stay with them!"

"But madam, he is *my* friend!"

"At once, missy!"

Surprised by the unusual command in her mother's voice, Margaret Weaver allowed herself to be bundled from the room.

"And do not interrupt us, else you'll displease me greatly," Beth called.

She closed the door firmly on the startled girl and stood for a moment, willing herself into calmness.

"So," she whispered, "after all these years, you have come . . . ?"

"By Jesu! Kit Wakeman!" Anne gasped, her face suddenly white. "You have no right to enter this house, sir, and you are not welcome."

"I didn't think I would be, Anne Weaver, but I will ever uphold my right to enter this house, for I have never ceased to regard it as my own."

He bowed again with exaggerated courtesy.

"And I think it would be best if you could use my other name, for it is the one by which my daughter knew me. I pray you address me as Cedric Woodhall!"

"Harry shall throw you out!" Anne threatened.

"I think not, since I know he is not here. Do not play games with me," Woodhall snapped. "Besides, my business is with my daughter. I would like to speak with her alone."

"There is nothing you can say that my lady may not hear," Beth insisted quietly.

"Ah, do not be too sure, daughter. There are things you cannot know . . ."

"There is nothing *I* cannot know," Anne quickly interposed. "If it is worth the telling, then I would like to hear it."

Woodhall flashed a look of undisguised pity.

"Then be it on your own head, Anne Weaver, for sins and chickens always come home to roost."

"Need we talk of sins?"

Desperately Anne played for time, silently praying that Beth would say nothing to goad Woodhall into anger.

If she tells him he is not her father, Anne thought wildly, if she faces him with the truth about Peter, then his vengeance will be terrible and the world will be told the truth of Harry's getting, of Meg's shame and of the lies John and me told. How then could she explain it to Harry and Beth, Anne fretted. Would Harry understand, let alone forgive, their deception?

Suddenly Anne's heart ached for the feel of John's hand in hers. She closed her eyes wearily, then opened them suddenly as she heard Beth's voice.

"My lady is right. There must be no talk of sins, no bitterness between us. Pray sit by the fire, father, and warm yourself? Are you hungry? Would you like a horn of ale?"

Relief flooded over Anne. Beth had understood. She, better

137

than most, knew Woodhall's violent temper. She would not risk arousing it when they were alone in the house with only children and elderly servants for company and the only men well out of earshot, sleeping above the stables.

"Beth is right."

Anne breathed more easily. "Since you are beneath our roof, it is only fitting to offer hospitality. Perhaps then you will tell us what has caused this visit after so many years?"

"Oh, I shall tell you, never fear." Woodhall was enjoying the confrontation. "But surely you can allow me the pleasure of sitting in my old home for a while? It is little to ask, surely?"

"Is that all you have come for, sir?" Beth demanded quietly. "Do you not want to know that my mother—your wife—died long since? Is my happiness of no interest to you, or my children? And where have you been these many years?"

"I have been living in France, daughter—I was given no choice . . ."

His eyes narrowed into slits and Beth was again reminded of the turbulence of his moods. Then just as suddenly he smiled.

He is like a cat that has been at a pan of cream, Anne thought. He has the air of one who knows he cannot lose. He is here to demand silence money.

If only it had been *his* head that festered over London Bridge, she wished. Strange that the rest of the world acknowledged him dead. If only the earth could open up and receive him—who would miss a man who died half a lifetime ago?

The idea was spawned with terrifying clarity. It hit Anne like icy water and it surprised her that she was in no way shocked by it.

Suddenly she felt a calm that lifted her body into weightlessness. She was no longer a part of the tight little drama being enacted in Beth Weaver's winter-parlour. She had stepped outside herself, a spectator all-wise and all-knowing. Suddenly she had the solution to the whole miserable mess. She said calmly, "Will you away to the kitchens, daughter, and bring ale for Master Woodhall?"

Anne's eyes sent out a warning as Beth, unwilling to leave the two of them alone, reached out for the bell.

Leave us, Beth, Anne's eyes said. *Give me a few minutes?*

"Very well, my lady."

Reluctantly Beth left the room.

"Be so good as to quietly close the door," Anne commanded Woodhall. Then, calmly confident, she said, "You want money? Am I right?"

The man looked up sharply, jolted out of his smugness by the directness of the old woman's approach.

"I want my rights. I am alone in the world, yet I fathered a daughter in wedlock and a son out of it. Can I not be allowed to satisfy my fatherly instincts?"

"God-damn you, sir, stop your sly hints!" Anne spat, hating him the more because she could not deny Beth to him.

"Tell me what you want before Beth is back."

"I want money. I want something of what is rightly mine!"

"So you are in trouble? By Jesu, but for the commotion it would cause, I would denounce you for what you are," Anne hissed.

Then she took a deep breath, fearful that they were wasting time.

"You shall have money and I will give you a horse that you might be out of my sight the quicker. But I need time so that it might be done in secret. I want Beth to have no part in this, you understand?"

"How much time? And how do I know I can trust you?"

"It will take me a couple of days to get a hundred

sovereigns together. As for the trusting," she shrugged, "you know I have no other choice but to pay."

Woodhall smiled and the evil in it made Anne want to puke.

"You are right, Anne Weaver. You have no choice and I accept your offer. It will do nicely for the time being."

Anne looked at him with contempt. He would be back again and again, she knew, demanding more and more. And soon the day would come when she was no longer there to pay and Harry would know—

In that moment she knew she was right in what she had determined to do. She said, "Very well; you must return two nights from now at an hour before midnight—I will leave the window of this room unlatched. Walk over the fields and through the wood so's the dogs do not get wind of you."

"And the horse . . . ?"

"I will make some arrangement about that tomorrow and tell you of it later. I cannot arouse suspicion . . ."

"By heaven, but you are a cool one, Anne Weaver," Woodhall's eyes narrowed in reluctant admiration.

"Oh, I can be cool." Anne raised her eyes to meet those of her tormentor. "I can be very cool, sir, when I set my mind to it."

The door-sneck clicked and Beth hurried into the room, carrying bread and cheese and ale. Her eyes slid from one to the other apprehensively, but she did not speak.

Anne smiled reassuringly.

"Thank you, Beth. Be so kind as to serve our guest so that he may be on his way."

Beth's forehead wrinkled into a worried frown.

"You are not staying, father . . . ?"

"No, daughter, not this time," he answered easily. "But I shall be back, no doubt. Perhaps next time I shall meet *all* your family."

Cold fury gripped Anne and she closed her eyes and willed herself to be calm.

By God, she vowed silently, but there will be no next time. I'll put an end to this cat and mouse!

She said nothing. Instead she thought about the potion cupboard in the cold pastry kitchen.

What shall it be, she pondered. Shall it be the nightshade or the monkshood?

She opened her eyes and looked at the man who sat at her table. She felt no pricking of her conscience at what she had decided to do, for no one could feel remorse at the putting-down of a mad dog or mourn a man who had long since died . . .

CHAPTER ELEVEN

HARRY WEAVER slipped from the back of his mare and looped the reins through the ring on the garden-door. All around him some of the cloistered peace of the priory still lingered, even though the soft measured tread of silent nuns no longer whispered along its corridors.

In the priory kitchens cooks and spit-boys sweated and stirred and spooned, determined that the meal they were preparing should be ready on time. But they had been given scant notice. Their master had set out from Bath before first light, yet the messenger who rode ahead to warn of his coming gave them little time in which to present so lavish a meal.

Perhaps Lord Mounteagle's kitchen servants would have been better served if that messenger had not first called upon his other master; if he had not stayed so long in Whitehall palace giving detailed accounts of Mounteagle's guests and the expected time of their arrival.

But Thomas Ward made a mockery of the adage that man cannot serve two masters. Master Ward served Lord Mounteagle and Robert Cecil with equal zest and scrupulous fairness. And when he had taken his leave of Cecil, those snippets of information he left behind him would be noted by Levinus Munck and faithfully recorded with all the other information concerning the priory in Montague Close.

Harry Weaver blew into his cupped hands. The weather was unusually cold, even allowing it was almost November, and the stars shone frostily in the clear night sky. At least, he thought, Mounteagle and his company should be able to make good time; there couldn't be too long now to wait.

It had been almost three weeks since he was summoned to Whitehall; three weeks of wasted time, for Harry Weaver would never understand the reason for that call.

He wondered, on his return to Aldbridge, just what he would say to Beth and the children in answer to their questions. How foolish he would sound when he said, "No, I didn't meet King James nor the Queen. I went all the way to London so that one night I might ride over the fields to Hoxton and deliver a letter!"

But he couldn't even tell them that, for once that letter left his hands, it was to be completely forgotten.

How he longed to be away from the intrigue. How he ached for the feel of Beth's soft body in his arms and the scent of rosemary on her newly-washed hair.

What wouldn't he give for the smell of wood fires and crisp autumn mornings.

In London everything stank: men, women, houses and gutters. Even the air a man breathed was tainted.

Disgruntled, he settled down to wait. The wind blew cold across the meadows at the back of the priory and he yearned for the comfort of his home. In the summer he had cut down old apple trees; they would likely be burning the sweet-smelling logs tonight in the small snug winter-parlour and Beth would be sewing in the candle-glow.

Harry's body throbbed with loneliness. He missed Beth intolerably, but most of all he worried about her, fearing for her safety, hoping she would have the sense to appeal to Jeffrey if she became afraid.

He swore impatiently; the sooner he was home the better. He had mentioned the matter to Master Munck only that morning, but he'd got nowhere.

"And I may leave as soon as I have done as you ask, sir?"

But Munck had havered and blustered and dropped his eyes.

"Ah, now, Sir Harry, that I cannot say. You should not have long to wait, though . . ."

"But Cecil told me I would be free to go once I'd safely despatched the letter."

"The letter, sir? What letter, pray?"

And so the silly game had started all over again, and they were talking in riddles and innuendoes, pretending neither knew the other and that letter in his jerkin pocket did not exist.

Why, he thought, should there be such a rigmarole about the carrying of a letter if all was honest and above board? Even the method a messenger used that morning was enough to make the whole thing stink like a midden.

"May I know your name, sir?" he had asked of the man who stood at the door of his lodgings.

"If I could step inside, Sir Harry—"

"Nay, I'll not open my door to a man who will not give me his name."

"Sir, I must have a care for the nature of my errand . . ."

"Are you from Cecil, then?"

The little man jumped as if he had been bitten, placing his finger across his lips, looking left and right and behind him.

"Oh, whisht sir, I beg of you!" His voice rose in a wail of torment.

"All right, then." Harry Weaver stepped aside. "But no tricks, mind."

He closed the door quietly and the soberly dressed man sighed audibly as the bolt slid home.

"Ah, Sir Harry, but you are a stubborn man. Were you

not expecting me? Had you forgotten you were to do my master a service?"

"If your master is Robert Cecil—yes, I believe I owe him a favour."

"Sir, let us not name names," the man whispered. "Sufficient be it that there is a letter—"

"Damn it, I've had enough of this cat and mouse!" Harry Weaver roared.

He was becoming sickened with the man's hedging. "I'll have your name, sir, since it is obvious you have mine. At least I'll know who I am dealing with."

"Very well—I had not intended you should know it. A man must have a care, these days, if he is to keep his head above water . . . It is Munck, sir; Levinus Munck."

"And you are in Cecil's employ?"

The grey little man shrugged.

"I serve King James."

"Then where is the pesky letter? Give it to me and let me be on my way, for I'm sick of all this play-acting."

"Forgive my natural caution, Sir Harry, but I had to be sure, you understand?"

He unfastened the pouch at his belt and took out a folded paper, half reluctant still to part with it.

"You are to take it to Hoxton. In Montague Close is a house that was once the priory of St. Mary Overie. It is a journey of about four miles and you must not arrive until after sundown. Be there about six of the clock so that you can deliver it immediately his lordship arrives."

"And his lordship's name?"

"It is William Parker, Lord Mounteagle, but you are not to give it to him. When Mounteagle and his guests have arrived, allow a little time for the commotion to settle, then take up your position by the front door."

"I am not to show myself . . . ?"

145

"No, Sir Harry. Make yourself scarce as you can," Munck confirmed doubtfully, looking up at the great bulk of the man, "and when a page comes out you will confront him."

"And will this page be expecting me?"

"No, sir, he will not, although he will have been sent on an errand by the one who *is*."

"Then . . . ?"

"Give him a coin and ask for Master Thomas Ward. But make sure your face is not seen. Pull your hat well forward and turn up the collar of your cape—"

A bird cried sadly into the darkness, sharply interrupting Harry Weaver's thoughts. It was an ill-omen when a night-bird cried above a man's head. He crossed his fingers and spat.

But the whole business was ill-favoured, he shrugged, and stinking with intrigue. The sooner he was out of it the better. He shifted moodily, chilled to his bones, hunching his shoulders against the wind.

"God-damn it!" he swore into the night. How had he gotten himself into such a fix? What gave Cecil the right to order him about like a lackey? By Our Lady, he thought angrily, but he'd get to the bottom of it, if he turned all London upside-down!

Levinus Munck had let nothing slip. The sly little clerk had refused to look him in the eye, coughing and spluttering, making excuses.

"You will hear from my master very soon, Sir Harry. I beg of you, do not take matters in to your own hands and leave London until he gives his permission."

"I'll wait a couple of days, that's all."

Just two days, he thought sombrely. If Cecil hadn't honoured his pledge by then, he'd go to Whitehall and be damned if he wouldn't bawl and rage until they were *begging* him to go!

Suddenly he lifted his head, ill-humour gone, fretfulness forgotten. They were a long way off, but the sound of riders came unmistakably clear on the still night air.

He stood up cautiously, stretching his cold cramped limbs, holding his head askew that he might better anticipate the direction of their approach. His countryman's ear told him there were about twenty horses and travelling at a great gallop as if sensing they were at the end of the road with warm stables and fodder a-plenty waiting for them.

His mare pricked back her ears and scraped the ground with her hoof, whinnying softly.

Now he felt a strange excitement as he was drawn still closer to the whirlpool of intrigue.

Cautiously he approached the front of the house, crouching behind a sheltering evergreen, hearing the riders' voices clearly as they called to each other above the din of pounding hooves.

Then they were clattering over the flagged courtyard and grooms and stable-boys ran out to help the riders dismount, unstrapping saddle-bags, leading the sweating beasts to the stables.

Harry shrank back against the light that suddenly streamed from the open front door, hating the deceit of his errand, yet reluctantly thrilling to it.

Soon the last of the horses was led away and the great doors slammed shut. All was quiet again, broken only by muted bursts of laughter or a voice demanding spiced wine and a page to pull off his boots.

Then, as he had been told it would, the heavy oak door creaked open again and a tall slim youth ran down the steps.

"Ho there, boy!" Harry hissed. "Has Master Ward arrived yet?"

"Aye. He rode ahead to prepare for my lord's arrival. Do you want words with him, sir?"

"If you'd be so good, lad," Harry replied gruffly into his neck-cloth.

He slid a silver coin into the boy's hand.

"Tell him I'll not keep him long."

"And who wants him, master? What name shall I give to Tom Ward?"

"It is of no matter, lad. Just take him aside and tell him quietly . . ."

The page pocketed his reward. Nameless strangers seemed always to be seeking Tom Ward these days. Be damned, he thought, but the fellow was popular.

Harry Weaver stepped back into the shadows. There had been about half a dozen men in Lord Mounteagle's party and several more servants. They had, he supposed, returned to London for the opening of Parliament, reluctant to interrupt their hunting but duty-bound, nevertheless, to do so. And like as not, when the pomp and speech-making were done with, they would toss their fine robes back into their cedar-wood chests and don their hunting leathers again. A man couldn't blame them either, Harry thought, the longing for his own familiar acres washing over him again.

A voice jerked him back to the cold earth of Hoxton.

"You asked to see me, friend? I am Thomas Ward."

Harry stepped forward a pace, hunching his shoulders into his cloak, squinting below the downturned brim of his hat at one who spoke with an endearingly familiar tongue. Damn it if Thomas Ward wasn't a man of York, an' all.

"Aye, sir, I am come from—"

He stopped abruptly. A man didn't name names when he handed over a letter that didn't exist.

"I am here," he hastily corrected, "to give you a letter for Lord Mounteagle."

"Aye, you are expected. Our mutual friend told me of you, this forenoon."

Ward held out his hand for the sealed paper, placing it carefully inside his doublet.

"Is that all, Master Ward? I may go now?"

Ward nodded.

"You have done what you came to do. There is nothing now to keep you here."

"Is there no reply to carry back?"

"*Reply?*"

Ward did not attempt to conceal the amusement in his voice.

"Reply, sir? Ha! You are a joker, an' all! No, friend. Before you know it, I'll wager this letter will be on its way back to he who sent it. Now forget you ever saw the letter— or me!"

Harry Weaver creased his forehead in exasperation. It seemed to him that to deliver a letter that was to be immediately returned to its sender was nothing less than a waste of good time and a task he could have well done without on so cold a night. But nothing about the whole business made sense, he shrugged.

"Your pardon, Master Ward, but for the life of me I cannot understand why—"

"Then do not try, sir. *You* are not meant to understand *anything.*"

Ward turned, his hand on the door-latch.

"And you are luckier than some. Indeed, it is a crying shame when Lord Mounteagle has ridden so hard that I must give him this letter and spoil his meal!"

He grinned, making lies of his words, for it was obvious

that the delivering of the letter would give him nothing but satisfaction.

"I bid you goodnight, friend," he said cheerfully as the door closed behind him.

"By Our Lady," Harry Weaver muttered, "be damned if I can make rhyme or reason of any of it."

He shook his head in bewilderment, a vague feeling of apprehension throbbing inside him like an uneasy tooth.

Something was afoot; some mischief spawned in high places at that. And whatever it was, he had been drawn into it, despite the fact that he had been repeatedly warned to forget every last detail of it.

"Damn it," he swore, "but I'll be made a fool of no longer!"

Robert Cecil, Harry reasoned, had chosen to involve him in something he had sworn was in the King's best interests. But if this was so, why couldn't the King's business be conducted in an open, honest fashion?

What secret scheme had Cecil thought up and why, fretted Harry Weaver, had *he* been involved? Surely Cecil had lackeys enough to do his bidding without entrusting so obviously important an errand to a man he hardly knew?

"Jesu," he vowed, "but I'll get to the bottom of this!"

He was angry now; angry at being treated like a gullible fool and angrier still that he had ever let himself become entangled with the whole unsavoury business.

He hugged his cloak closely around him and pressed his body into the shadows again.

So the letter was to be returned to the sender? Then it wouldn't hurt if he were to wait a little longer and see if Master Ward's prophesy proved true or false. After all, he had nothing better to do. What was there to lose?

The devil himself must have been hard on the heels of the

man who hurtled through the front door of the old priory, belting on his rapier and calling for his horse as he ran.

There was an excited murmuring behind him and men were talking in an excited babble as they followed him down the steps and into the courtyard.

"Demand to see Cecil . . . !"

"Aye, Will, have a care!"

Will? Was this man then William Parker—Lord Mounteagle? Was this the man to whom the mysterious letter had been addressed and was he, as Master Ward had predicted, returning it to Cecil?

But why in heaven's name should it be returned to Cecil? He must know its contents word for word. Why then was Mounteagle nearly breaking his neck in his eagerness to get it back to him?

Only one thing would satisfy him now, Harry Weaver decided. As soon as he safely could, he would follow the rider who threw himself astride his horse as if his life depended on it. It would probably do no good, for the chances were he'd lose his quarry in the darkness. But the letter was on the move again and he reckoned he had the right to know where it was going. It had caused him enough bother and that gave him fair reason to be interested in its welfare, he decided.

He could still hear the retreating hoof-beats as he unhitched his mare's reins.

"All right, my beauty."

He patted the elegant arch of her neck, then gave the creature her head and she was away, fleet and silent as a shifting moonbeam.

Lord Mounteagle was a troubled man. If, he reasoned, the letter was as dangerous as he feared, then the sooner he reached Robert Cecil with it, the better.

Why, he fretted, should he of all men be singled out to be

the recipient of such news and why would the danger to himself be passed once he had burned the letter?

By Jesu, but he would do no such thing! The letter was going straight to Cecil, Mounteagle vowed, jabbing his horse in panic-stricken urgency. He wanted rid of it, for it seemed that it sat there like a red-hot coal, ready at any minute to burn a hole right through his pocket.

The letter could well be a test of his loyalty, he reasoned, and if that were so, then he was doing what any loyal Englishman would be expected to do. Cecil should have no cause to regret the trust he had placed in William Parker!

With a sigh of relief, he saw the great dark bulk of London ahead of him, stark against the starlight and wreathed in a haze of coal-smoke. He had never before been so glad to see it and he closed his eyes, praying that the man he sought would be there, working at Whitehall still.

He leaped from his horse, tossing the reins to one of the soldiers who stood guard at the door.

"Lord Mounteagle to see the Earl of Salisbury," he snapped, walking past them with such an urgency that neither of them dared bar his way or ask his business.

"Only let him believe my innocence," Mounteagle whispered as he strode along the familiar corridors that led to Cecil's quarters.

"Let him not doubt me?"

The Earl of Salisbury had dined well and now he sat with his guests, enjoying a rare pipe of tobacco, for King James's absence at Royston enabled them to indulge in such a pleasure. Only when His Majesty was in London were pipes and tobacco jars tucked into hiding.

Cecil lifted his glass to his lips, enjoying the fine Portuguese wine.

The fingers on the clock that stood on the side-table pointed to nine o'clock and soon, if his plans were not to be upset, the peace in that room must surely soon be shattered.

He did a mental calculation; allowing Mounteagle a reasonable ride from Bath and provided Harry Weaver had done as he was bid, it shouldn't be long now.

He glanced at his guests, noting with satisfaction that his best wine had been well squandered. Their features were relaxed, their smiles mellow. They would be receptive to anything he might suggest.

It was important that there should be reliable witnesses to hand when Mounteagle—or Mounteagle's man—was shown into his presence. Who more reliable than the Lord High Chamberlain, the Lord High Admiral and the Earls of Worcester and Northampton?

He relaxed in his chair, quietly confident that all would go well and almost as he had envisaged, the door of the room crashed open.

" 'Pon my soul! Mounteagle!"

Cecil jumped to his feet, his face registering the exact amount of surprise and annoyance.

"God's death, man, is the devil after you?"

Lord Mounteagle's face was taut as he handed the paper to Robert Cecil.

"I pray you do not joke, my Lord Salisbury, for the devil, if he is not after me, might well be the cause of yon' mystery!"

He nodded towards the letter.

"Read it, my lord—"

His eyes were still wide with fear as Cecil's guests, their state of blissful inertia disturbed beyond redemption, sat bolt upright in their chairs and puffed rapidly at their pipes.

"By the Lord Harry, what have we here?"

Cecil reached for his spectacles, slowly hooking them round

his ears, holding the letter to the candle-flame with irritating slowness.

His brow creased into a dramatic frown and his eyes popped wide open.

"What's this, Mounteagle? Who sent you this letter, eh?"

"My lord, I do not know," came back the anguished reply. "It was given to Thomas Ward, one of my gentlemen, by a man who would not give his name. I brought it at once to you, sir, for I want no part in it!"

"Hmm. Quite right, Will Parker."

Cecil studied the letter dramatically.

"What's this? . . . *as you value your life, find some excuse to absent yourself from the opening of this Parliament—*"

Cecil looked around him in triumph. Then he continued to read.

". . . *Parliament will receive a terrible blow and they will not know who hurts them . . .*"

He shook his head in deep distress.

"Gentlemen, I fear that good Mounteagle has been presented with something that is most dreadful to contemplate."

He handed the letter to the Earl of Worcester.

"Read it," he commanded. "Go on—read it aloud!"

The Earl of Worcester did as he was bid, his face darkening with rage as he read, and when he had finished, the room was gripped by a stunned silence of disbelief.

Then Mounteagle spoke.

"My lords, I swear to you I know nothing of these terrible implications nor am I aware of the identity of he who wrote the letter or he who delivered it. I am innocent—"

Robert Cecil smiled placatingly.

"Nay, good William, do not fret. None here have any reason to doubt your loyalty. You acted correctly and in the best interests of His Majesty; I commend you for it."

He poured a goblet of wine and placed it in Mounteagle's agitated hands.

"Take a sip of wine," he soothed, "for your health's sake. You have nothing to fear, my lord; nothing at all."

Inside him, Cecil felt a satisfaction that warmed him through.

He picked up the letter and eyed it dubiously, as if he had never until that moment set eyes on it.

Levinus Munck had made a good job of it, but then, the little clerk always made a good job of such things. Master Munck, Cecil acknowledged yet again, was worth his weight in rubies.

Carefully he locked the letter in his desk, hard put to it to keep the smile of sheer joy from his face.

"Well, gentlemen," he sighed. "What's to be done, do you think?"

CHAPTER TWELVE

ANNE WEAVER hobbled painfully around the small room, praying that none of those who slept upstairs would be roused by her clumsy movements.

The shutters were closed against escaping candlelight, but soon she would slip the window-catch so that Kit Wakeman, when he came, might enter the house without being seen or heard.

Carefully she set two of her finest goblets on a silver tray, then lifted the lid of the wine ewer into which she had poured some of her best wine, making sure the amount was exactly enough to fill the goblets, knowing none must be left for some unsuspecting person to drink.

From the small money-cupboard set in the chimney breast, she took a leather pouch and a small earthenware bottle. The pouch held a hundred carefully counted sovereigns; the bottle was ordinary—similar to the one in which she kept the essence of vanilla she always added to her syllabub. Curiously numb, as though it held nothing more hurtful than carefully hoarded flavouring, she shook it, wondering if her wicked mixture would do what she wanted it to do, marvelling at her complete lack of feeling.

It had been easy to get the henbane, for she always kept some in the potion-cupboard, one small drop a sure remedy for sleepless nights.

But the distillation of monkshood had been harder to come by, for it was the most deadly of poisons. It was strange that

Harry should have bought some only recently to put down a hound gone mad with pain.

Now she had need of what was left of it; wasn't she too putting down a mad dog?

Carefully she poured the mixture into the ewer, shaking the bottle to release every last drop. Then she hurled it into the hearth, closing her eyes as the fragments shattered in all directions.

Slipping the pouch into the pocket of her dress, she hobbled to the window and unhooked the catch, setting her lips grimly to stop their trembling.

She had made her peace with God and there was nothing more to be done but get the matter over with.

She sat down, willing her thoughts away from what was to come, wanting only for the time that was left to think of precious things.

Her hands stroked the arms of the chair. Once it was John's chair and she had found great comfort since he died by sitting in it. Tonight, more than ever, she longed for his hand in hers.

She closed her eyes, shutting out the present, willing herself into a past in which she had been happy, thinking desperately of John.

She had always loved him; she couldn't remember a time when she had not. Her loneliness had been almost unbearable since he died.

But John's death had been the Stuart's fault, she thought childishly. If John hadn't gone to York . . .

Always, Anne thought bitterly, a Stuart had been at the bottom of all her heartbreak. And they had unthinkingly called the babe Anna. They had given her a Stuart's name and she had known then that no good would ever come of it.

Once, Anne had hoped to die shriven with God's name on her lips. Now she was not so sure.

Perhaps it might make dying all the easier if she were to use her last breaths wisely; use them for the cursing into eternity of all Stuarts.

She shook her head. She must not be unhappy when time was so precious. She must remember the good things; John's slow, shy smile and Meg's dreaming eyes; the farmhouse by the green, the loom and the fire-oven.

She would think of Yuletides past and haytime and harvest and Goody Trewitt's sad old face.

And when the end came, Anne thought, would John come to her, his hair thick and brown again, his back straight and his body whole? Would he stand with outstretched hands and help her to take that last tremendous step?

"John love," she whispered. "I am afraid. Be near me?"

A twig cracked sharply beneath the window and Anne's eyes jerked open. Slowly she rose to her feet. There was no going back now.

Slowly she pulled aside the window hangings, then walked back to her chair.

"So you have come?" she said.

The man Anne had been reluctantly expecting climbed carefully through the open window.

"Did you hope I wouldn't?" he asked, his mouth drawn down at the corners. "Did you think to get away with it so lightly?"

Anne shrugged.

"No, I did not. There is always a reckoning-day."

"You are wise to admit it, Anne Weaver, but I am in a hurry."

He thrust out his hand.

"Where is the money? Did you get it?"

"I did and you shall have it. But will you give me your word that you will not bother me again? Will you go away and not come back?"

Anne's tormentor leaned indolently on the mantel as if the house and all in it were his again.

"I will not bother *you*," he said softly.

"And Harry? You'll let him be, an' all?"

"If I gave you my word on it, you'd not believe me!"

"I would like to try," the old woman pleaded.

The man shrugged his shoulders indifferently, refusing to answer.

"Did you think you would not be found out, Anne Weaver?" he hissed suddenly. "You let them marry, *my* son and *my* daughter; they are blood-kin and living in incestuous sin!"

Anne closed her eyes, willing her tongue to be still, clenching her hands tightly in an effort not to fling the truth in his face.

But she is not your daughter! she longed to taunt him.

Then she took a deep breath. It didn't matter now; let him think what he wanted to think. She had been foolish to hope he would go away and leave them in peace. He would never let it rest. He would be back again demanding more and more money, for even if he discovered the truth of Beth's fathering, there was still Harry's secret.

She said, "At least take wine with me before you leave?"

"If you will drink too, Anne Weaver."

"I will," she nodded, pouring the wine, waiting for him to take whichever goblet he chose.

"You said you'd give me a horse?"

"Aye, and there is a gelding in the small paddock at the back of the stables and a saddle by the white gate. It will be up to you to get the beast away without rousing the horseman or the dogs."

"I can easy do that," Wakeman retorted, ungraciously.

"Where will you go?"

Even now, Anne wanted to give him one last chance.

"I don't know," he shrugged. "I must leave England for a time, for Wakeman was condemned for rising against Elizabeth Tudor and Woodhall is a wanted man still."

Then he lifted his eyes to hers and smiled as if he knew something she did not.

"But the time will come, and very soon, when I shall be able to come back openly and claim justice for my wrongs."

His words seemed like a threat almost, confirming Anne's secret fears. Defensively she lifted her chin.

"Then I wish you luck of it, master; I shall not care what becomes of you. And do not think I could ever forgive the way Meg died!"

"Do as you like, old woman," he mocked. "Either way I have you in a cleft stick. But if you do not betray me, your nastly little secret will be safe."

"For as long as I pay, eh?"

Wakeman turned his back, choosing to ignore the question, lifting his goblet to his lips.

"Are you going to drink with me?"

Oh, I'll drink with you, Anne thought, taking the other glass. *God help me, I have no choice now.*

She took a long, slow sip and was relieved to find the drink was still palatable.

She drank again, willing him to drain his glass. Only let him do that, she prayed.

"Here is your money," she whispered, tight-lipped. "Take it and go!"

Wakeman took the pouch as if it were nothing but his due.

He is evil, Anne thought, and without shame. Could it really have been he who fathered so fine a man as Harry? Could one so wicked beget someone so good?

He tossed down the last of his wine and Anne closed her eyes with relief. Now she only wanted him out of the house and as far away from Aldbridge as it would be possible for him to ride. She said, "I will not wish you God-speed, for you are evil and the devil's mark is on you. But when he has taken you, may you know a little of the purgatory you have caused others to live through."

"You speak as though we shall not meet again, Anne Weaver," he taunted, a smile of malice on his lips.

He stepped up to the window-ledge then turned on his haunches to face the old woman.

"I shall not bid you goodbye, for it is likely I will be back!"

He laughed softly, then swung himself down to the soft turf of the lawn outside.

He was still laughing as he walked away.

Anne closed the window quickly, then returned to John's chair, pressing her trembling body into it. She looked at the goblet in her hand, then took a deep breath. She didn't want to finish her wine, but she must pay a life for a life . . .

As she set down the empty glass, her hands were trembling and tears of fear filled her eyes.

"John, my love, what have I done?" she whispered to the empty room. "Pray for me that the Almighty will grant me understanding?"

Then she felt a calm begin to wrap her round and knew the worst was over, for the room felt pleasantly warm and a drowsiness pricked at her eyes and made her limbs feel heavy. She wanted to think about Meg and John, but there was something still to be done.

Her finger-tips and toes tingled with a strange cramp; time was precious.

Desperately she gathered in her thoughts.

"Mary Stuart," she whispered, "I curse your soul into eternal damnation. May it never rest in peace and may those who served your cause rot stinking at hell's gate!"

The room was tilting giddily and Anne Weaver's body seemed no longer to be her own.

"Mary Stuart," a strange voice echoed above Anne's head, "I curse you and all those of your ilk both dead and living and still to be spawned. May they never know contentment. May they know what it is to see the children of their bodies snatched away by death. May all Stuarts weep, as I have wept . . ."

For a moment terror gripped the old woman. I am dying, she thought wildly. I am living through the loneliest moment of my life!

"John?"

Her stiff lips formed his name. She was afraid and she wanted him near her.

She forced open her tired eyes, peering into the gloom.

He was standing there and his hair was thick and brown again, his back straight. John had come for her. He was smiling and holding out his arms and Anne's body felt free again as it had done in her youth.

Tenderly she smiled into the beloved face . . .

Kite Wakeman cursed the mist that shifted before his eyes. His head felt light and his hands were numb as he tried to keep a hold on the reins. It had taken him a long time to saddle up the gelding, for his fingers seemed suddenly to have grown useless.

Now he approached the top of the hill and the cross-roads that stood outside Aldbridge village, blessing himself against the evil that lurked at every crossing of the ways.

He glanced to his right and saw the sturdy oak that stood opposite the gibbet-elm. John Weaver had planted that oak; it was an open secret. He had done it to protect Meg's grave.

So long ago, Wakeman's befuddled mind supplied. So long

that it was over and done with. She couldn't have him now, in spite of what she had whispered from her death-bed.

He remembered the night he had asked for her forgiveness. He had been about to ride out and do battle for Mary Stuart and it was important to him that his soul be cleansed, for no priest of his own faith had been in the district for many weeks.

But Meg Weaver's mutterings were those of one who is in her death-sleep.

'I will come again. One day, in another life, I will have you. Wherever you are, I will find you, Kit . . .'

Of all his women, she was the one he remembered best. She had loved him and given her eager body without restraint. Her hair tumbled the hay as she lay beneath him and her lips had been soft and warm.

He closed his eyes tightly, then opened them again, staring into the shifting darkness.

He gasped and shook his head, willing the face before him to be nothing more than a figment of the inertia that was fast taking hold of him. He lifted his hand to his eyes and it felt heavy and useless as his tongue that seemed to be swelling until he wanted to choke.

The face was nearer now and he saw the sad blue eyes and the hair that drifted on the night-mist like palest spun gold.

'Kit, my love, you have come to me . . .'

Damn it, she should not have his soul! He dug his heels into his horse, trying to urge it away, but his limbs were useless.

The wraith was blocking his path, her hands held out to him, her eyes begging him to come to her. On her face was a look of unspeakable love.

The gelding snorted with fear, his ears pricked back, his head thrown high.

"Mother of God," Kit Wakeman jerked, "is she real? Has the beast seen her too?"

He tried to shout to her to go away, but he could not. Desperately he tried to keep his seat as the reins fell from his useless fingers.

The horse whinnied, a half-crazed scream of animal terror, then reared itself up, its hooves flailing madly at thin air, afraid and uncontrollable.

I am falling, Kit Wakeman thought wildly.

His body hit the earth with a dull thud. He stared upwards, incapable of movement and dizzy with fear. He saw the underbelly of the horse and thrashing, crashing hooves.

There was a vicious blinding pain in his head and the feel of warm blood on his cheeks. He tried to shield himself, but could not move and besides, all was dark now.

He heard Meg's voice again, calling him softly, "*Kit, sweet love, come to me?*"

He smiled, for the pain had gone and his body was light as air. It was Childermas again and Meg's hand was inside his and they were running laughing, across the snow-covered cobbles of the stable-yard . . .

*   *   *

Robert Cecil sat back contented and awaited John Johnson's arrival. He had gambled outrageously and he had won, he exulted. He had bided his time, playing out the rope of intrigue inch by inch until now it was long enough for a hanging.

Last evening, the Earl of Suffolk and his troopers, together with Sir Thomas Knevett and poor frightened Mounteagle, had searched the coal-cellar beneath Parliament House and what they found there had completely justified the months of waiting and worry Cecil had endured. Beside a great heap of coal and firewood, they found Thomas Percy's servant, guarding, he said, his master's winter fuel stocks.

He had been able to tell them little, save that his name was John Johnson, but then they found a pocket-watch in his possession—and what servant, Suffolk reasoned, owned such an expensive luxury—and a tinder-box, touchwood and a slow-match in the pocket of the jerkin beneath his smock.

So the searchers became more suspicious and Knevett had hog-tied Johnson with his own garters and sent the poor protesting fellow under escort to the Tower, doubtless thinking that a night in that miserable fortress would loosen the man's tongue and help jog his memory.

It was then they found the powder, thirty-six barrels of it, enough to blast Parliament House and all inside it to certain oblivion.

It was all Cecil had been waiting for. Now he would be able to cease his string-pulling and manipulating, for all that remained was to despatch a band of troopers to Royston to escort King James to the safety of his capital.

"Mercy on us, Robbie, who would want to blow up his King?" James Stuart whispered incredulously when told of the facts of the momentous findings. "It's against God's law to harm the person of one of His own anointed," he said, conveniently forgetting the illustrious precedent of his own mother's end. "I canna' believe it; I say, I canna' believe it!"

He asked then that John Johnson be brought to Whitehall so that he might talk to him and learn the truth of Percy's dreadful treachery.

Poor frightened James, thought Cecil gleefully, trying hard to compose his face into mask of serious contemplation. Now the King would believe all he had been so carefully told about the disloyalty of Romanists; now he would listen more carefully to the wise words of his Principal Secretary.

Cecil allowed himself the smallest of smiles. Like as not,

King James would now be sitting in his chamber, nibbling his finger-nails and flinching at every creak of the floorboards.

Cecil jumped startled to his feet as the door burst open. "Who are you, sir? How dare you enter my room?" he demanded testily. Then he swallowed hard and let go a sigh of relief, for the intruder was Harry Weaver.

Nevertheless, some unsuspecting guard would be given the fright of his lift for allowing it, Cecil vowed as he lowered himself trembling into his chair again.

"What do you want, Sir Harry, and who let you in?"

"I am here to demand that I be allowed to go home, sir," the irate man retorted, "and I got in by picking up the guard outside your door and throwing him along the corridor!"

His face was red with rage as he towered above the puny little hunchback.

"Pray calm yourself, Sir Harry. Brawling is not tolerated in the King's palace!" He shifted uneasily. "And come to think of it, how did you get into the palace?"

"I told the guards I had urgent business with the Earl of Salisbury an' that's the truth, for I'm sick of kicking my heels in this city!"

"By God, sir, I like your cheek," Cecil retorted reluctantly, "but I am taken up with the King's most important business today. Come back another time," he added, making a mental note that in future any guard who let Sir Harry Weaver within a hundred yards of the palace of Whitehall should swing from the nearest gibbet.

"No, my lord. Here I am and with respect, here I stay until you give me leave to go home. I cannot leave my wife and mother alone any longer . . ."

He stopped and shrugged, resignedly.

"If I may not return home, I ask that you give me a good reason why I may not."

Belligerently Harry Weaver stood his ground.

"Reason, sir?" Cecil spat. "I don't give reasons to anybody! And mind your tongue, or I'll call the guard and have you flung into the Thames!"

Harry Weaver grinned, his good humour returning.

"Then best call good and loud, my lord," he retorted, "for the one who stood outside will be of little use for a time!"

"You are a rascal, sir," Cecil sighed defeat. "What am I to do with you?"

Weaver was of the salt of the earth, he had to admit it. He would make a good servant for King James. It had been foolish to doubt his loyalty and there was nothing to justify keeping him in London any longer, he had to admit.

If only the northerner could be pressed into service, he fretted, what a splendid acquisition he would make. A man of Weaver's calibre could be of untold worth in watching the comings and goings of the wild northern counties.

"If only I could be sure of your allegiance, Sir Harry," he sighed, his eyes fixed on his hands, "if you could make but one indication of your loyalty to King James and myself, there would be nothing to stand in the way of your return to Yorkshire this very day!"

"But I *am* loyal, my lord. I did as you asked. I delivered the letter exactly as your man instructed."

"The letter, Sir Harry? I know of no letter!"

"All right, I take your point, my lord. But let not you and I play games?"

There was an urgent knocking on the door and Levitus Munck burst into the room, his face flushed, his eyes shining with suppressed excitement.

"He is here, my lord," he panted. "They are bringing him up the stairs. Johnson has come!"

From far along the passage came the measured tread of heavy boots. Cecil followed Munck to the door, waiting expectantly, clasping and unclasping his fingers, glad of Harry Weaver's towering presence despite the fact that Johnson was in the care of two troopers.

The captain of the escort bowed.

"I have the man Johnson from the Tower, my lord."

Cecil nodded.

"Wait here a while. His Majesty will be informed."

Then he turned to Harry Weaver, speaking urgently and quietly.

"I can spare you no more time, sir, but come back tomorrow or the next day. Perhaps then we can come to some understanding—"

Harry Weaver's face flushed with anger and he turned abruptly from the foxy little man who seemed to shift this way and that as the wind bent him. Then he looked up and gasped in amazement.

"By the Lord Harry, it's Guy Fawkes!"

The man in the smock of a servant dropped his eyes to his boots and spoke quietly.

"Sir, you are mistaken. I am John Johnson, a servant. We have never met before, you and I."

Harry Weaver roared with laughter.

"Nay, Guy, there's no need for play-acting here. You need not pretend you do not know me, for like as not they'll want nothing more serious of you than to deliver a letter that doesn't exist or some such trifling escapade!"

He held out his hand in greeting.

"Just do as Lord Salisbury says, Guy, and if you're lucky he'll let you be away home to Scotton again."

He roared with laughter, thinking that Whitehall palace must surely be as mad a place as Bedlam Hospital.

Robert Cecil's nostrils quivered like a ferret after blood and his eyes met those of his clerk.

Fawkes? they signalled. *Then we know this man?*

Munck affirmed with the slightest nodding of his head that the name could be found in the secret records of Cecil's archives.

Cecil's heart beat with a surge of triumph. John Johnson be damned! Here was one of the Romanists mentioned in Beelzebub's report and so cleverly exposed by Harry Weaver.

"So you are Guy Fawkes, a soldier who fights in the Low Countries for Spain; a known Romanist?" he gloated, scarcely able to disguise his elation. "Be damned if you'll not tell me what's to do in Mistress Skinner's coal-hole, Master Fawkes, else we'll find a way of helping your memory!"

Harry Weaver grinned.

"Take no notice of him, Guy. Little curs always yap loudest. His bark's worse'n his bite!"

But the man who called himself John Johnson shook his head sadly.

"By Jesu, Harry, I'd never have thought you'd sell yourself to Cecil," he said as he was hustled away.

Harry Weaver stood in blank amazement.

"Who would have thought to meet an old school fellow in the palace of a King?" he mused. " 'Tis a small world, eh, my lord?"

"I must be away, Sir Harry, but I thank you for the expression of loyalty I asked of you."

He smiled and took out a pouch from the table-drawer.

"You did it very cleverly, my friend; very cleverly indeed."

He nodded then winked with deliberate slowness.

"You will find in the future that I am always grateful for favours."

He walked to the door.

"I must go to the King, though 'twill be interesting to see what kind of a tune Master John Johnson will sing now, eh?"

He held out a cold, clammy hand.

"I wish you God-speed, Sir Harry, and a safe journey to York. We shall meet again soon when this business is done with and Romanist pigs have settled for their treachery. I think you will be able to serve me very well friend—very well indeed."

With that he was gone, his elated feet fairly dancing along the polished boards of the long passage.

Harry Weaver stared at the money pouch.

"What did I say," he whispered, "that is so deserving of such reward?"

He had joked about Guy's presence and then he had looked into his sad eyes and seen fear there and despair.

The money felt heavy in his hand and he remembered the story of a man named Judas.

"God in heaven," he whispered. "What have I done?"

CHAPTER THIRTEEN

"HELL's teeth!" gasped Sir Harry Weaver's horseman. "It looks as if a mad dog's been at his face!"

He swallowed the spittle that rose in his mouth.

"What happened?"

"I'm not sure, Gideon," Jeffrey Miller shook his head, "but I'd say his horse threw him then trampled him—there's blood on one of its hooves."

The horseman turned his back on the mutilated face and walked to the waggon that was piled high with sacks of flour.

The horse had been hitched to the back of it.

"Look for yourself," Jeffrey invited.

"Jesu, but that's the missing gelding!" Gideon gasped. "I left him in the small paddock, but this morning he'd gone—slipped his tether. I thought nothing of it—he's a wild one and he's broken loose before—but then I found a saddle gone, an' all!"

He spread his hands in a gesture of disbelief.

"Well, a runaway horse don't saddle himself . . ."

"So you think yon' fellow took it?"

Jeffrey nodded his head to where the dead man lay.

"Seems likely, Master Miller."

"And then the beast threw him, I suppose. If the man had been set about by footpads, I'd have understood it, but his horse and money are still there, so it looks like an accident."

171

"He took the beast good and quiet, for I didn't hear him," Gideon pondered. "Who is he, anyway?"

"I don't know," Jeffrey lied flatly.

"Then what's to be done with him? There's trouble enough at the manor house without adding to it."

"Trouble?"

"Aye. It went clean out of my mind. I was riding after you to bring you back—Lady Beth is in need of you. They found Lady Anne dead this morning."

"*Dead?*" Jeffrey hissed.

"Aye; sitting in her chair."

"But she seemed in good fettle yesterday—"

Jeffrey Miller's heart thudded dully. "What happened? Was there foul play?"

"From him, you mean?"

Gideon glanced at the inert body at their feet. "No, she hadn't been badly used. I saw her myself. She died at peace for there was a smile on her face as if she was glad to go."

Jeffrey closed his eyes and shook his head wearily, saddened beyond belief. Lady Anne had been his true friend and he loved her dearly.

"Don't take it badly, master," the horseman was well aware of the corn-miller's special relationship with the Weavers. "She was a good age. There's not many spared to live out their three-score years and ten."

"It's a sad loss, for all that. And what of Sir Harry? It'll be a bad blow for him, when he returns."

"More's the pity he's been gone so long," Gideon nodded, "for the Lady Elizabeth'll have to see to things on her own."

"Then I'll be getting back. Give me a hand with this fellow, Gideon."

It would be best, Jeffrey decided, to take him to the big house. He had died on the manor and he was the manor's responsibility. And there might be someone at the manor-house who could throw light on the subject; explain, perhaps, why the man was riding one of Sir Harry's horses and carrying one of Lady Anne's money-pouches.

Together they slung the body over the horse's back face downwards, the hideous mess that was once a face hidden from passers-by.

Jeffrey unhitched the gelding.

"Lead him back slowly, Gideon. The beast knows you and he'll not play you up."

Carefully he turned the waggon round. There would be no going to market now. With studied carelessness he asked, "Have you seen the fellow before?"

"Can't rightly tell, master; not from his face, anyway," he shrugged, "but there has a been a man with hair like his skulking round the big house and eating from the dole-cupboard. Once I saw him sitting in the lane at the back of the stables, talking to Mistress Margaret."

"But you don't know his name or where he might be from?"

"As far as I'm concerned," Gideon shrugged, "he's a roadster—a vagrant."

Jeffrey let out a small sigh of relief. With luck the truth could be kept from Beth. If they could get him shrouded in cere-cloth and decently buried before any of the manor-house servants had time to see him, perhaps Harry's wife could be saved a lot of heartache.

But luck was not with them, for Father Goodbody was taking his leave of Beth as they approached the house and there was nothing to be done but bluff it out.

"He's only a vagrant, Father," Jeffrey answered when the fat little priest demanded to know what was to do.

"I found him by the cross-roads; reckon the horse threw him. His face isn't a pretty sight, so I'd not advise you to look on it," he added hurriedly.

"No, Master Miller, death is rarely pretty, but I have need to look upon it constantly," came the smooth reply. "Vagrant or not, he is entitled to my prayers."

"Prayers for a horse-thief, Father?"

Jeffrey was glad of Gideon's indignant protest.

"He had the missing gelding with him, my lady," Gideon appealed to Beth, "and a good saddle!"

Jeffrey heard the sharp intake of Beth's breath and wondered if the sight of the dead man or the recognition of his red hair had been the cause of it.

But she said nothing, only continuing to stare at the lolling body as if she could not pull her eyes away.

"A horse-thief, you say?" clucked the priest. "Is that so, my lady? Has the fellow made away with one of your horses?"

"Yes, Father," Beth nodded, "it is one of our beasts."

"Then you may do what you like with the felon, Master Miller, for he'll not receive absolution from me nor rest in my churchyard. There's little enough room there for honest Aldbridge folk!"

"Then what's to be done with him?" Gideon demanded.

"Take him to the cross-roads. Take him anywhere—I don't want him or the expense of burying him out of the Parish Chest!"

And so proclaiming, the man of God stormed away, his Christian charity reserved for those more deserving of it.

"Put him in one of the stables, Gideon," Jeffrey said quietly, "and cover him over. I'll see to him tonight."

Mutely they watched as the body was borne away, then Beth turned to Jeffrey, her eyes wet with fresh tears.

"I thought I had cried myself sick for my lady," she whispered. "I never thought I'd have a tear to spare for *him*."

"You know who he is, then?"

"Yes, Jeffrey. I don't need to see his face. I knew he was here, anyway."

"Then why didn't you send for me? I'd have seen him off for you!"

Beth Weaver shook her head wearily.

"He's been about the place for a long time. Two days ago he came to the house. I think Lady Anne offered him money and a horse so's he'd go away. Perhaps she gave them to him last night."

"Aye, my lady." Jeffrey held out the money-pouch. "I found this in his pocket. It's one of Lady Anne's. Best lock it away again."

Absently Beth took it, her hands agitated, her voice trembling with tears.

"Oh, Jeffrey, I'm so confused. I can't seem to think straight."

"Then I will stay with you for a while," Jeffrey comforted. "Gideon can drive the waggon back to the mill and tell my Judith where I am."

Beth nodded, her face set in distress.

"Come now, my lady. I pray you not to grieve. Lady Anne had a good life—Gideon said her passing was peaceful. She missed Sir John sadly. Try to think of them as being together again."

"Oh, I've tried, but it's not that easy. I fear for her soul, God forgive me. I fear she may have condemned herself to eternal damnation!"

Jeffrey placed his comforting arm round Beth's shaking shoulders and gently led her into the house.

"Tell me?"

"Come into the winter-parlour. There is something you must see, Jeffrey."

She pointed to the goblets.

"Someone came here last night and took wine with Lady Anne."

"And . . . ?"

"It was Master Woodhall—or Kit Wakeman, whatever." Beth whispered.

"When he first came to the house, Lady Anne sent me out of the room on an errand. I think she arranged then for him to return without my knowing. He came in by the window, for there were marks on the sill and the floor beneath. I rubbed them out."

"Then it's all right, isn't it? Your father wasn't a thief."

"He wasn't my father, Jeffrey. I thought you knew!"

"I did, my lady. Sir John told me, long ago. It was just a slip of the tongue, that's all."

"You know *all* about him? And about *me*?"

Jeffrey nodded.

"Then tell me what you make of this?"

She opened a drawer and took out a cloth in which she had wrapped the fragments of a broken bottle.

"I found it shattered in the hearth. I think it was thrown there and deliberately broken. I think it contained . . ."

She shook her head, her eyes searching Jeffrey's for courage.

"My lady," he interposed. "I know what is in your mind, but do not say it. Do not even think it. What happened to Kit Wakeman doesn't matter. He died many years ago as far as most folks know, so how could Lady Anne's soul be at risk?"

"It's not as simple as that. Jeffrey. Lady Anne took wine with Woodhall, so she also drank . . ."

She shook her head, unwilling to say the word.

"Jeffrey, our lives belong to God—we none of us have the right to say when we shall end them."

"And you think Lady Anne took her own life? Nay, my

176

lady! I cannot believe it. It is too ridiculous to even think about!"

"You truly believe that? Upon your word of honour?"

"Aye, I'd swear to it! Lady Anne died at peace. Wasn't she smiling?"

Damnation, he thought savagely, suicide or not, none should hang *that* label on her whilst Jeffrey Miller lived and breathed.

"So say no more about it, my lady, not even to Sir Harry, eh?"

"Yes, Jeffrey, you are right," Beth nodded, relieved beyond measure.

"Tonight I shall bring my waggon and since Father Goodbody will not have any truck with Wakeman, I'll lay him at the cross-roads. Perhaps of your charity, you'd pray for him?"

Then the kindly man turned sharply on his heel and walked quickly away.

For Meg's sake he'd do it. Meg had died calling for Kit Wakeman. Now she could have him, Jeffrey vowed grimly. He would lay her lover in the earth at her side and her tormented soul could rest easy.

"God help me," he muttered, "but this has the makings of an awful day."

*　　*　　*

Guy Fawkes stood stiffly between the halberdiers, glancing about him, noticing ordinary, everyday things in a world turned suddenly topsy-turvy.

The floor on which he stood had been swept and waxed and the fire that crackled in the hearth lit as part of an ordinary day by an ordinary lad who would now, most likely, be eating his dinner with a dozen other lads.

But for himself, thought the prisoner, things would never be ordinary again, for he had plotted high treason against

177

his King and was discovered; he had masqueraded as a servant and was betrayed. Now he awaited a confrontation with the man he wished dead.

Sitting unspeaking behind the long narrow table was Robert Cecil and beside him a drab grey clerk with quills, paper and an ink-jar at the ready.

There were other men of rank too—the Lord High Chamberlain and the Lord High Admiral, splendidly dressed to the height of their officialdom, and the Earls of Northampton and Worcester, travel-stained as though they had not long tumbled from their horses. Men, thought Guy Fawkes, who had just done ordinary things like sleeping in a bed or eating a good breakfast.

"I will have faith," he silently vowed. "Mother of God, let me not disgrace myself?"

There was a stirring at the table and the doors at the far end of the long chamber were quietly opened.

Guy Fawkes turned his head and raised his eyes and looked at James Stewart.

He saw an uneasy man who was ugly and puny with close-set eyes, a mean mouth and a large, bulbous nose. Even the splendour of his clothes did nothing for him, save to make him look the more ordinary by comparison.

Was this then a King, the son of a Queen, chosen of God to rule divinely by his own right?

No, this could only be the persecutor of Romanists, the lover of small boys, the man who could defile the carcass of a slain deer. This creature was beneath contempt, of no more worth than that which the cat left stinking on the midden!

Charles James Stuart lifted his head high, thinking that the room down which he walked seemed a mile long. He had still not recovered from the terrible news with which Cecil had confronted him; could not yet accept that there existed even one man who could connive at the death of his King.

178

And why was the wretched man not cowering on his knees, blubbering for mercy? How dare he look upon the King of All Britain as if he were of no more importance than a mangy cur?

He gave his head a defiant toss. Did it matter what the great ruffian thought?

It was a fact, James Stuart acknowledged silently, that Robbie Cecil had been right all along. He should have listened more closely to him.

Lord have mercy, he thought, I could have gotten myself killed! It would have happened to me just as it happened to my poor, wronged daddy!

The thought sent his legs into violent spasms of trembling and he was glad to lower himself into his chair and nod to his Principal Secretary to start the questioning.

But Cecil's probing was of no use, nor were his soft suggestions, worthless promises or threats of a cruel, violent end.

The man they had thought to be a servant and of little consequence had proved to be a soldier of skill and bravery, a fanatic Romanist already known to Robert Cecil and his spies.

This man resisted Cecil with unspoken contempt, maintaining quietly that he was John Johnson, servant to Thomas Percy, and that he and he alone had intended to blow up Parliament House.

"But did ye not know that ma wife would be there too and the Prince of Wales?" the King interrupted indignantly, unable any longer to remain aloof and apart.

"Would ye have killed them an' all? Would ye have killed ma lords and bishops? What have *they* done to harm ye?" he squeaked.

"They have done nothing," replied Guy Fawkes gently, "and their deaths would have been regrettable."

"And *me*? Do ye not know ye canna kill a king?"

"But the Pope has excommunicated you, James Stuart. I could have killed you with an easy conscience."

"The *Pope* excommunicate *me*? I don't know what ye're blethering about, man."

The prisoner sighed. He had not expected the King of England to be so stupid.

"Each Maundy Thursday," he explained softly as if he were reasoning with a small child, "His Holiness casts out all those not of the Church of Rome. You are a heretic, so you were excommunicated. I could have killed you without endangering my immortal soul."

James's mouth sagged open, his sparse squat beard seeming to tremble with shock.

This prisoner before him was not afraid! He was calm and quietly defiant. God rot him, James Stuart swore, the man was looking at him with a contempt that was frightening.

"Man, have ye nothing to say? Can ye not offer one word of regret, one jot of shame?"

"No, I cannot. My conscience is clear. I owe no allegiance to you, James Stuart. You are not of my faith and I do not consort with heretics!"

The King opened his mouth again and his eyes popped amazement.

"Who is in this with you?" Cecil snapped, taking up the questioning again. "Tell us the names of your fellow conspirators that it may please the King to deal the more lightly with you."

"There are none in it, save myself."

"You lie, fellow. There are others. We know their names and can take them at once. But you will help yourself by confessing your guilt and denouncing those who plotted treason with you!"

Guy Fawkes shook his head with gentle exasperation.

"There are none," he insisted softly.

"Then tell me of Thomas Percy, the man you say is your master? Tell me of Christopher Wright, with whom you were seen in Ripon and—"

He stopped, biting back Harry Weaver's name. For once, Cecil admitted, the agent who kept his finger on the throbbing pulse of northern intrigue had been wrong.

Weaver was loyal and he had proved his loyalty by cleverly denouncing the man who was standing before them now.

Cecil permitted himself a small, secret smile. By now the great bluff Yorkshireman would be heading for home and grateful beyond measure for it, no doubt.

"Do you deny knowing that those men are Romanists?"

"Sir, I cannot deny nor confirm it. I have no knowledge of the faith of the men you mention."

"You lie!"

Fawkes shrugged his shoulders in a small, helpless gesture.

"No, my lord, I do not, but if it is Romanist blood you're after, then I am your man. I am not ashamed to confess my faith if it will please you."

Cecil turned triumphantly to Levinus Munck, who wrote laboriously at his side.

"You are noting all this, Master Clerk? You have it writ down that this man is a confessed Papist?"

Munck nodded, unspeaking, his pen racing rapidly across the paper.

"And what of those others, Master Fawkes, who came to Whinniard's tenement?"

"Others? I know of none, save my master who had every right to be there."

"Liar! There have been many men visit that house who remained there for several hours at a time. What were they doing? Did they hear Mass and receive absolution for their plotting against King James?"

The prisoner shook his head, stubbornly mute.

"What did they plot at Whinniard's?" Cecil demanded yet again.

He longed to play one of his trump-cards, but knew he dare not. He could not confront the man with his knowledge of the gunpowder or tell him that it was known how many barrels had been taken from the Tower and rowed to Lambeth. How it would have shattered the calmness of the arrogant one to hear it.

But he must not, for to have done so might well have revealed his prior knowledge of the plot. It might, even, have brought to light the fact that men suspected of plotting to kill their King had been deliberately allowed to rent a house and cellar in dangerous proximity to the home of the King's Parliament, or that Robert Cecil, closest of all men to the King, had given it his blessing!

But the eager little hunchback was not unduly worried. There was still Mounteagle's letter which would serve equally as well, Cecil reasoned, warming to the unqualified success of the episode. No one, he exulted, would ever know the source of such a master-stroke of double-dealing. Munck who helped in its preparation and Tom Ward who had seen to it that things went smoothly at Hoxton, were tried and true servants. Even Harry Weaver who reluctantly and innocently delivered it, now seemed to have realised which side his bread was buttered on.

"Answer me!" he demanded. "Men came to Whinniard's and you must know of them! What were they doing?"

"No men called at Whinniard's, save those who had the right to do so," came back the dogged reply.

"Ha! You have changed your tune, Master John Johnson. Who were the men?"

"There was the milk-seller, my lord, and the coal-heaver and the apple woman, aye, and the Pope and the Spanish Emperor!"

"Enough!" Cecil yelled, his face red with rage.

"I think you do not fully appreciate the gravity of your position. Do you not know that in the end all men tell us what we want to know?"

Oh, yes, and I shall tell you too, Guy Fawkes thought sadly. *It was not for nothing that I was accidentally taken to the secret cellar where men, after a time, are glad to answer all questions.*

How long would he be able to stand up to it, he wondered; for how long could he be brave?

He knew about William Wade and his skilled persuaders; knew of the heated stones, the Scavenger's Daughter and the rack.

Would there, he thought, be black-hooded torturers in that cellar and a surgeon to see to it that they did not quite kill him? And would it not be better if they were to kill him in that secret place beneath the Tower, for wasn't the ultimate penalty for treason far worse?

What mattered was that he should be able to hold out for just long enough. He cared little if they knew every one of the thirteen conspirators. Catching them would be what counted.

If I can hold out for two days, Fawkes thought, they can be down the Thames and halfway to Flanders. Maybe even now, they were well on their way to safety.

He tilted his chin higher.

"Mother of God," he prayed silently, "for just two short days, give me the courage of a saint?"

*   *   *

Jeffrey Miller threw his spade back into the waggon and rubbed his hands down his jacket, stamping flat the earth at his feet as he did so.

"That's it, then, Gideon. Father Goodbody doesn't want the fellow, so we can only do our best for him."

"Should we say a prayer, do you think?" Gideon suggested apprehensively. "It's a terrible thing to have to be buried at a cross-roads."

"Perhaps we can prevail upon Father Goodbody to give him absolution later on," Jeffrey suggested.

A sack of flour, no doubt, would do the trick . . .

"We have done all we can. Let's be away, Gideon, for it's dark and cheerless here."

For the life of me, thought Jeffrey, I could not say a prayer over yonder grave. How could I, when I'd have his soul in purgatory as soon as blink?

He straightened his shoulders, then climbed onto the waggon.

"Two deaths in the parish," mused Gideon. "Will there be a third, do you think?"

"No, I don't," Jeffrey replied firmly.

But for all that, he thought, he wouldn't be sorry when Sir Harry's London business was over and done with.

"Let's be away," he said again, for it was nearly midnight and that was reason enough. Such places at such times were best left to the restless dead.

He clicked his tongue and brought the reins down hard on the horse's back, thinking of his soft feather-bed and Judith sleeping there, safe and warm.

Suddenly he felt weary for rest. Things wouldn't seem half bad in the morning—they never did.

He shook the reins again as a hunting owl ghosted above them and crossed his fingers and spat as a man always did whenever he saw the great white bird.

"Damn it, Gideon, but I'll be glad to be abed," he said, smiling into the darkness. "And show me a man who's not in his bed at this ungodly hour and I'll show you a fool!"

There were fools a-plenty in London and two such men sat late in the palace of Whitehall.

"My, but this has been a terrible day," whispered James Stuart. "I can scarce believe it, e'en yet."

"Then put it from your mind, Sire," comforted Robert Cecil, supremely confident, "for you are safe now."

"What'd I do without ye, ma good and true servant? Had it not been for you, I'd have been with my Maker this night and my wife and son with me!"

The watery eyes stared into the glowing coals.

"And poor Elizabeth and wee Charles just fatherless puppets in the hands of those Papists! By the Lord God, I have been over-trusting to a fault!"

"That you have, Sire, but the wrongdoers will be punished."

"Aye, but where are they? Away to France, I shouldn't wonder."

"I think not," Cecil gloated. "In my opinion they are all still in England and cheeky enough to try to raise an army against you, Sire."

"But they'll not succeed, will they? My people wouldn't take up arms against me, surely?"

"We shall see to it that they *don't*!"

"And how will ye do that, man?" the King fretted, "when ye don't know for sure just who ye're looking for?"

"Not for sure—not yet—but I'd hazard a guess that Thomas Percy is in it up to his neck and Master Catesby, an' all. And it won't be long," he smiled, "before Guy Fawkes will tell us all about the rest of them."

"Then the sooner we can make an example of them all, the better!"

"Oh, we shall do that all right," Cecil whispered. "There are no degrees of guilt, to my mind. They who plot against your Majesty are all equally guilty—all of them traitors."

"So, Robbie?"

"So Fawkes will do as well as the next man. I do not think he is the ringleader, but we have him so he will be our arch-villain. Let Fawkes be our scapegoat."

Aye, let the people see how near the Romanists had brought them to disaster, thought Cecil. Frighten them, whip them into a fury, post notices, issue proclamations, set neighbour against neighbour if needs be, but *discredit all Romanists*! Sow fear and mistrust and so arrange it that not one Jesuit priest was left alive in England to spread his doctrine of hatred!

Now was the time to rid the country of Papists for all time, he vowed savagely. He would never again have such an opportunity.

"Well, Sire? What say you?" he urged.

"Ye are right, Robbie, as ye always are," nodded the King sadly. "The man Fawkes will do as nicely as any."

He rose unsteadily to his feet.

"Call the guard, will ye, so he can escort me. I'd like now to be away to my bed."

But for all Cecil's precautions, for all the doubling of guards and ravening mastiffs that roamed the palace gardens, James Stuart lay stiff with fear in his bed that night and heard the watchman call every hour until it was light.

He sighed and glowered at the burly trooper who had replaced the page-boy who usually kept watch at the foot of his bed.

Things would never be the same again, he sighed. Dear God, but who would be a king?

CHAPTER FOURTEEN

THE apple logs that glowed in the hearth smelled as sweet as Harry Weaver imagined they would on that cold night in Hoxton. Now, unbelievably, he was home and all was quiet save for the small sounds that always beset an old house when it sleeps.

He sighed and thought of Beth. She had gone to bed alone and almost gladly. Something is wrong, he thought irritably. There had been a cloud over his homecoming and Beth was taut as a coiled spring.

There had never been secrets between them, yet now he was measuring each word before he spoke it. He wanted to tell Beth about the London visit and what had happened there.

I think you will be able to serve me very well indeed, friend . . .

What would she have made of Cecil's cryptic remark and what, if he'd told her about it, would she have done with the pouch of gold that had been thrust upon him? Dare he tell her about the favours that had been slyly hinted at—favours Cecil would *always be grateful* for? Could he admit that the recognition of an old school-fellow had become a terrible betrayal?

And why, he fretted, gazing into the flames, had Margaret's outburst left Beth more agitated than before?

He knew his Beth so well; she would be lying dry-eyed in the darkness now, thinking as he was thinking that this was not the way she had planned his homecoming should be.

187

What had happened in his absence? He had asked the question of Beth the moment he leaped from his horse and gathered her hungrily into his arms.

"You are all right, my darling—truly all right?" he breathed. "You are not harmed?"

And when she asked him what prompted such fears, he shrugged his shoulders with studied unconcern.

"Oh, I heard as I rode through the village that some ruffian had been seen around the house and that a horse-thief was found dead at the cross-roads."

"Yes, dearest, that is so, but Jeffrey saw to it. You see," she hesitated, "other things have happened . . ."

She told him then of his mother's death and they held each other close in their grief, all else forgotten.

And later, sitting quietly in the fire-glow—too quietly, he thought now—the door had hurtled open and back with a shuddering crash.

"Margaret!"

Beth jumped to her feet.

"Why are you not in your bed? And fie, miss, for parading about the house in your sleeping-shift. You are not a child to tumble about the place half dressed," Beth scolded.

"Madam, this evening when I wanted to talk to my father, I was a child and it was past my bedtime . . ."

Harry held out his hand.

"Then come and talk to me now, sweetheart," he said, smiling in spite of himself at the sheer exuberance of her.

"You spoil her," Beth fretted. "And why did you come downstairs, Margaret? Have you a belly-ache?"

"No, madam. I couldn't sleep for thinking about the man they buried at the cross-roads."

Harry glanced at Beth and a face that was suddenly alert with fear.

"What about him?" he demanded. "What's it to you, missy, that it should keep you awake nights?"

"It is a great mystery to me, sir. Why was the man taken at night to the cross-roads and not buried in the church-yard?"

"You want to know over much," Beth retorted, fear sharp in her voice. "The man was a thief and Father Goodbody wouldn't have him. And what is so strange that a cross-road burial should take place at night?"

"Then why did Gideon deny knowing him? *I* knew him!"

"*You*, Margaret?"

"He was my friend. He sometimes came to the dole-cupboard and we met and talked in the lane. And you know him too, my lady, for he came to the house!"

"Go to your bed at once," Beth hissed, her mouth dry with apprehension.

"Don't be hard on the little maid, Beth. Let's hear what she has to say. I don't like her choice of friends, but by heaven, I like the way she defends them! She shall go to bed, love, when she has told me about this man."

Gently he took the girl's hand in his.

"Are you sure it was your friend they buried at the cross-roads?"

"Yes sir, I am. They'd covered his body and said we must none of us go to the stables, but I went. I didn't see his face, but I saw some of his hair. It was red and my friend's hair was red . . ."

"You're sure about that, Margaret?"

The teasing indulgence in Harry Weaver's voice was gone.

"Yes sir, and it was all over curls, like yours!"

For a moment that seemed like an eternity there was silence in the room, then Harry said quietly, "Best do as your mother bids, daughter. Be off to your bed."

There was authority now in her father's voice and Mar-

189

garet Weaver knew better than to argue, and her mother's face was white as a bed sheet, she thought anxiously.

Quickly she bobbed a curtsey and scuttled away, glad to leave the room where the air was thick was unspoken accusations.

"You knew, Beth? You knew who the horse-thief was?"

Silently she nodded her head.

"It was Christopher Wakeman, wasn't it? The man you knew as Cedric Woodhall."

"Yes."

Her acknowledgement was little more than a whisper.

"I asked if you were safe and you said nothing. What happened when he came here to make you lie to me, Beth?"

"Nothing happened, Harry. I just didn't want to add to your grief. And anyway, it was Jeffrey who found him. He knows more about it than I."

"Jeffrey! Jeffrey Miller'll be taking over the running of the manor 'ere long, I'm thinking!"

Beth spun round, stung to rare anger.

"Jeffrey is a good friend and he was here when I needed him!"

"And I wasn't . . . ?"

Then she ran to him, arms outstretched.

"Let's not quarrel, husband. Woodhall isn't worth it!"

He held her to him, loving her and wanting her.

"You're right, love; he's not important—not to us, at any rate. But Cecil seems to think otherwise. Cecil knew Woodhall was here in Aldbridge—that's why I was worried about you."

Beth was still desperately afraid. She took a deep, calming breath, then said, "It's true he came to the house. I only saw him once, but I'm certain he came again, secretly. Your mother gave him the horse I think and money, too. He didn't steal anything and I don't think he harmed my lady, either."

"He was a traitor, Beth; don't try to defend him!"

"I'm not. I just want you to know that your mother died peacefully."

"Did he say anything?" Harry shrugged. "Anything of importance, that is?"

"No, but I think he was desperate for money. And he thought still that I was his daughter; we didn't tell him different."

She puckered her forehead.

"But why should Cecil know of his movements?"

"I don't know," Harry lied. "And besides, Woodhall's dead now, so it doesn't matter, does it?"

Beth had gone to bed then, pleading a sick headache, and Harry was reluctantly glad, for Jeffrey would be coming soon and there were things to be said that were not for Beth's ears.

Damn Cecil, Harry thought viciously, and damn Woodhall, too, for the unrest they had caused between Beth and himself. Things had come to a pretty pass when a man came home after a month's absence and his wife took to her bed with a badly head!

He rose to his feet and piled logs into the hearth, then filled a goblet with wine, tossing the liquid down his throat as if it was ale.

Be damned, he thought savagely, if I don't empty the bottle!

But Jeffrey Miller's arrival saved Harry from the miseries of a thick head. Somehow, just to see the great bluff man calmed his anger.

Jeffrey held out his hand, a smile of pure pleasure on his face.

"Thanks-be you're back safe, Sir Harry. I'm sorry to intrude on your first night home, but I wanted you to know about Wakeman—"

"Aye, Beth has told me about it all."

Jeffrey drew sharply on his breath, wondering how much he knew, hoping with all his heart Beth had been discreet.

"At least, I think she has told me all, Jeffrey. She seems a little strained . . ."

"My lady has been through a lot lately; perhaps that would account for it. She knew Wakeman was around the place—even before you left for London, Sir Harry."

"Then why didn't she tell me?" Harry exploded.

"I asked the same thing. She simply said she hadn't wanted to worry you."

"And do you think the man harmed my mother? If I thought he'd been in any way the cause of her death—"

"Nay, Sir Harry. Lady Anne died at peace, be sure of that."

God in heaven, Jeffrey prayed inside him, forgive me my lies?

Then he shrugged his shoulders, for not for anything would he voice his suspicions to Harry Weaver. Lady Beth had said nothing, it seemed, so neither would he. Nothing should be allowed to taint Lady Anne's memory, he vowed.

Harry was quiet for a moment, then suddenly he said, "I'm glad to be home, Jeffrey. 'Struth, yon' London is a frightening city to be in."

"Aye, I know it. But tell me, sir, what of the Papists and their plotting, eh? Is it true, then?"

"You know about it, Jeffrey?"

"Aye, not half an hour ago. A rider on his way to Ripon stopped at the inn. The whole village is buzzing with the news. *Is* it true?"

"I reckon so, but I only know what I managed to glean on the ride home. I knew something was wrong before I left London; by the time I'd reached Selby, I'd got the whole story. By God, but bad news travels fast!"

Then carefully leaving out what had happened in London,

Harry told all he had been able to learn about the plot to kill the King; of the posters he read on his homeward ride that denounced the traitor Fawkes and named Thomas Percy as a fellow conspirator. And by the time he'd ridden through Leicester and Nottingham and Selby, the story had become a whole lot clearer.

". . . and when I got to York this morning, a King's messenger had ridden in just before me. It seems there were thirteen in the plot and four of them Yorkshiremen. That'll do us no good up here, I'm thinking."

"And are they captured, these men?"

"I heard so and that two had been shot by the Sheriff's men. Talk had it that Percy was one of them."

He shrugged.

"I suppose the bullet is kinder and quicker."

And he heard, too, that the prisoner Fawkes had held out for three awful days against the most fiendish of tortures, refusing to name his fellows, taking the whole guilt upon himself.

And his courage was wasted, Harry thought bitterly, for instead of fleeing the country, those conspirators Fawkes tried so bravely to protect had fled north and straight into the arms of Sheriff Walsh who waited near Stourbridge.

Poor brave Guy, Harry mourned silently. Friend of my youth, forgive my betrayal?

Then he shook himself. It was too late now for regrets. He smiled sadly.

"What's afoot, Jeffrey? There's things about my visit to London that puzzle me. At first, Cecil thought I had a hand in the plotting, but I convinced him of my loyalty in the end."

"*You?* Bound up with Romanists? Damn it, I'll not believe that!"

"Cecil did," Harry smiled wryly, "and you couldn't blame

him. Woodhall was up here; Cecil knew all about Woodhall in fact, right from the time he was Kit Wakeman and rose for Mary Stuart."

Jeffrey stiffened and his mouth went suddenly dry.

"But what's it to you, Sir Harry? Are you to be held responsible for every felon who walks over your land?"

"You'd think not, but Cecil had the look of a man who knows the answers even before he's asked the questions."

"I don't follow you."

"Then think on this, friend. I am summoned to London for no reason that I can think of, then accused of being a Papist-lover. I am asked trifling questions, then suddenly it's hurled at me, right between the eyes!"

He paced the hearth, fighting to control his anger.

" '*What do you know of Christopher Wakeman?*' Cecil flung at me. It was as if he was trying to shock me into admitting something."

"And what did you tell him?"

"What could I tell him, save what everybody knows!"

Harry shrugged impatiently, then demanded suddenly, "Wakeman had hair like mine, hadn't he, Jeffrey?"

"He had, but why do you ask?"

"Because Cecil kept on and on about it. I tell you, you'd have thought the fellow was my kin and I was being asked to account for his wrongdoings."

"*Kin?*"

"Aye, but Cecil always called him *Wakeman*, not Woodhall, and it was all a mix-up of hints and sly digs. I've thought about it until my head spun, and I can't come up with an answer."

"Then why try, Sir Harry?"

But there was a sick feeling in the pit of Jeffrey Miller's stomach. Cecil knew the truth of Harry Weaver's getting, he thought dismally. Elizabeth Tudor had known it. What more reasonable, then, that Walsingham should have known—and now Cecil?

"I must get to the truth. It was something Cecil said as we parted that has me foxed."

He refilled his goblet, pouring another and handing it to Jeffrey.

"I'll tell you what I think Cecil is up to, Jeffrey, and when you've heard me out, maybe you can help. But it's a strange story . . ."

He shrugged.

". . . You see, I think Cecil wants me. He's got spies everywhere—it's no secret. There's likely been one of them round Aldbridge, else how could he know what he does? Anyway, when I left him he hinted that he and I would work well together. There was no *By your leave, Sir Harry*; he was very sure of himself. I think he's going to try to force me to spy for him, Jeffrey."

"How can he force you—?"

"I don't know. Maybe there's something he knows that I don't. Perhaps that's the way he works—'*Do as I bid you, or else* . . .' "

"And what hold could he have over you?"

"I don't know. But before long he's going to summon me to London again, I know it."

"And you'll go?"

"I'll have no choice, will I? Who dares defy Cecil?"

"Then would it be such a bad thing to be in Cecil's good graces?"

Jeffrey was bothered and he knew the knowledge Robert Cecil would use. Wise old Sir John. His words came back to Jeffrey now, their meaning suddenly unmistakable.

". . . *if it happens that Harry should need to know the truth of his parentage* . . ."

"Well, Sir Harry, *would* it be so bad?"

195

Harry Weaver's face flamed with anger.

"By God! You think I'd sell myself to yon' devil in London? Do you think I'd betray my fellows, Papists *or* Protestants? I thought you knew me better'n that! You're like all the rest, Master Miller! You'd lick the muck off Cecil's boots for just such a chance, eh?"

He stood stiff with anger, his eyes blazing.

"Why don't *you* make haste to London, eh, Jeffrey? Cecil's looking for a good lick-spittle from these parts. Away and offer yourself to him. Sell *your* soul for a pouch of sovereigns!"

He stopped short, panting for breath, his face contorted with hate.

Slowly Jeffrey Miller rose to his feet, then setting down the goblet he held, he lifted his great fist and brought it crashing into the angry face before him with all the cold, calculating force he could muster.

Harry Weaver's head jerked back; his hand flew to his face and his eyes narrowed into vicious slits.

"*You struck me!*" he hissed. "By God, I could have you flogged . . . !"

"Aye, I struck you. But I'm not your vassal. My land is my own and I'm a free man. Sir John saw to that!"

"Then why . . . ?" Harry whispered, all anger suddenly gone.

"I did to you what I'd have done to my Diccon, rest his soul, or any son who spoke to me as you did."

"*But I'm not your son, Jeffrey Miller!*"

A look of infinite pity came into the older man's eyes.

"No, God help me, but you might well have been, for I loved your mother with all my heart."

"*You?* Loved my *mother?* Are you gone mad?"

"No lad. And I think that when I struck you, I was looking into another face, for in your hatred you looked just as he once looked."

"Like *who*? Hell, man," Harry Weaver's voice rose to an anguished cry, "tell me what you're on about?"

Jeffrey smiled gently.

"You don't want to work for Cecil, do you?"

Harry shook his head.

"Then when he sends for you, tell him nay."

"How can I, Jeffrey? There's something Cecil knows."

"Aye, and you'll know it an' all, so you'll be able to take the wind out of his sails. Tell him that although your father might have been a traitor, there's none of his badness bred in *you*!"

"By Jesu, you go too far, Jeffrey Miller. John Weaver was the best man who ever lived!"

"Aye, and I loved him too."

"Then what . . . ?"

Almost involuntarily, Harry Weaver touched his hair.

"Red curls, like mine? Kit Wakeman—*my father*?"

Jeffrey nodded, saddened beyond belief by the misery in the other man's eyes.

"And my mother whom you loved, Jeffrey?"

"Meg, my love-pledge."

"It's true?"

The world was rocking beneath Harry Weaver's feet.

"You wouldn't tell me false, Jeffrey?"

"No, Sir Harry. But don't fret, for Wakeman lies at the cross-roads now, and the only one who knows about it is me."

"But how did they keep it quiet? How did they get away with it?"

"I don't rightly know. I was working away at Skelton on my uncle's land, or I suppose I'd have known sooner. Old Goody Trewitt put the story round that Meg's mother was with child and very sickly with it, because of her age. Of course, folks thought it natural that Meg should stay by her bedside constantly—they believed it, anyway. But for all that, it must have been a worrying time for them all. It was a small miracle, I reckon, that it turned out as it did."

"And Meg died at my birth?"

"No. There was a mob of beggars in the village, demanding food. They turned on Meg when Kit Wakeman said she was a witch. She died not long after you were born—her head was injured, you see ..."

"And did Wakeman know?"

"No, not until that day. They managed to keep it from him, an' all. I found Meg lying there—the day I came home from Skelton ..."

Jeffrey's eyes took on a remembering look and his voice dropped to a painful whisper.

"I'd a length of blue silk in my pack for her wedding dress and a ring ..."

He shook his head, remembering the pathetic rain-soaked body and the fear in Kit Wakeman's eyes as he stood over it.

"The beggars had all run away, frightened at what they had done. Meg bled, you see, when they stoned her, and they knew then that she wasn't a witch. So I picked her up and carried her home. It was lucky she was wearing a long cloak —it covered her body completely, so no one knew."

He shrugged.

"The villagers had barred their doors and pulled in their shutters against the beggars—no one saw anything. By the time they finally crept out of doors again, it was all over and Meg safely indoors."

"And they buried her at the cross-roads?"

"Aye, the old priest was scared of his own shadow. He was afraid of any suggestion of witchcraft, you see."

"And I was brought up as John Weaver's son?"

"Aye, Goody found you a wet-nurse. She said the shock of Meg's death had robbed Lady Anne of her milk."

"It was a rare deception, Jeffrey."

"And if it was—what of it? Elizabeth Tudor knew of it and it didn't cause her many sleepless nights, I'll be bound. Reckon she took great delight in giving Kit Wakeman's lands to you!"

Jeffrey smiled encouragement, for he'd dealt Harry Weaver a body-blow and he was still reeling from it.

"Just before Sir John died, he released me from my oath of secrecy. He thought that some day you might need to be told."

"And that's why you've told me now, Jeffrey? You think Cecil will use it to press me into service, eh?"

"Aye, I do. He'd know of it. Like as not there'll be a record of it somewhere in London."

"And Cecil would be bound to ferret it out," Harry Weaver shrugged, his voice bitter.

"Well, at least I'm prepared. And he'll send for me, make no mistake about it. Once the business of Guy Fawkes is over and done with, my Lord of Salisbury will be casting around for fresh mischief."

"And you'll say him nay, Sir Harry? You'll not do Cecil's dirty work for him, for all he can put it around that you're . . ."

He stopped, unwilling to say more.

"That's I'm a traitor's bastard, you mean? No, Jeffrey, be damned if I'll do his bidding!"

"Then good on you, Sir Harry! Mind, there's some might twitter a bit when they hear about it, but I reckon it'll be a nine-day wonder. You'll get over it!"

Then a great sadness came over the miller's face.

"But for all that, I'd like to have spared Sir John's reputation. He was a saintly man and I'd not like folks to condemn him or Lady Anne for doing what they only thought to be right."

"And they shall not be condemned, Jeffrey, nor Meg, for I think I can put paid to Cecil's hash!"

Suddenly he grinned confidently.

"You think you can get away with it?"

"I know I can, Jeffrey. I can't tell you about it, but . . ."

Then he threw back his head and laughed out loud.

"By the stars, he'll not have it all his own way with me!"

Then he was serious again.

"I haven't rightly taken in what you've told me, but the more I think on it, the more sense it makes. You're a true friend, Jeffrey Miller, and I can find it in my heart to wish that next to Sir John, you had been my father."

He shook his head, bemused still.

"It's going to take a bit of getting used to, Jeffrey."

"Aye, but once you've accepted it, you'll find that nothing's changed. Don't fret on it over much; take it bit by bit—"

Jeffrey smiled his slow gentle smile.

"It's late, Sir Harry, and I'm for my bed. If you've any sense, you'll push the whole thing to the back of your mind—until the morning, at least."

"Aye. Beth'll be awake still, I suppose. What do you think she'll say to it all, Jeffrey?"

"Why tell her? What good would it do? And besides, I'd be damned if I'd waste time talking about my parentage—tonight of all nights!"

They stood at the front door for a time, looking up at the frost-ringed moon that hung low in the November night.

Harry held out his hand.

"I shall not forget your goodness, Jeffrey. I know now why my father and mother—"

He stopped and smiled.

"—why Sir John and Lady Anne loved you so. And if I

ever get over big for my breeches at any time, think of me as your son, if you will, and cuff my ear again!"

Then he turned and bolted the heavy old door behind him.

He felt sad and glad, proud and humble, and his body ached for the comfort of Beth's arms.

"She'll be awake, still," he whispered to himself, "and sad because on my first night home there is unhappiness between us."

The feather bed would be soft, he thought, and Beth's body warm and gently yielding. She would hold out her arms to him and he would bury his face in her soft hair. There would be no need for words.

"Beth," he called urgently, taking the stairs two at a time.

Jeffrey paused by the great wooden water-wheel that turned his mill-stones, looking back across the green and up the hill towards the cross-roads where Weaver's Oak stood black against the palely-lit sky.

Just one week ago he had lain Kit Wakeman there at Meg's side, giving back in death he who had spurned her in life. Now her soul could rest contented or wing away to some little Eden where reunited lovers find peace again.

Strange, thought Jeffrey, how lonely, how deserted the oak tree looked tonight. But Meg was gone now. She had waited, yearning softly for her long-ago love, and now they were together.

From the first flowering of her womanhood she had loved only him; she had given her body for the bearing of his child and called to him with her last breath.

Now Kit Wakeman was hers. He, Jeffrey Miller, had given him back to her and there would be peace again around Weaver's Oak. Tonight John Weaver's tree was cold and barren in its winter sleep, but come summer it would live again, green and lush as was the way of all things, and nightingales would sing in its topmost branches and the heartsease bloom again at its roots.

Jeffrey turned and walked slowly towards the door of his houseplace. It was long past midnight, but a candle still burned in the window.

He smiled. Judith was waiting for him.

EPILOGUE

THE great bell had stopped its tolling and the watchers who clung to every pinnacle and buttress of Westminster Abbey reluctantly scrambled from their positions of vantage.

Now the Palace Yard at Westminster was deserted, save for the small wizened man who brushed the square and a tall, broad man who stood unmoving in the deepening dusk.

Best not to clean up too well, thought the man who wielded the broom; best leave something behind. The crowd that assembled to watch the killing of the last of the Gunpowder Plotters had been a vast one, but there must surely be many who missed the fine day's sport and would want to come on the morrow and gaze at the spot on which the Papists had met their end. Best leave something for them to see—blood, perhaps, and a little gore.

He tucked his broom under his arm and picked up his lantern.

My, he thought, but it had been a rare day. It would be a long time before the citizens of London saw its like again.

Harry Weaver stood silent and still as the light from the street-sweeper's lantern bobbed into the distant darkness, swallowing hard on the spittle that swamped his mouth, wanting for the hundredth time that day to spew the contents of his belly to the ground at his feet.

Since early morning, Londoners had had their sport, applauding the arrival of the black-hooded hangman and his assistants, cheering like men possessed when the fire for the burning of the entrails was lit, eyes wild with anticipation of what was to come.

Then, almost with pomp, two men carrying a butcher's block had solemnly entered the enclosure, followed by the butcher himself, eyes hidden behind a black mask, brandishing his ugly cleaver like a play-actor.

They had behaved like animals, Harry Weaver thought. He had wanted to leave; to push his way through the ravening crowd and see nothing of the carnage that was to come, but he willed himself to stay. I must be there to pray for Guy Fawkes, he thought. Someone must speed his soul on its way— it is the least I can do for him.

Four men died that day—Winter, Rookwood, Keyes and Fawkes, the others having been despatched on the previous day outside the big gate of St. Paul's churchyard.

At the Palace Yard, Harry Weaver missed nothing of the slaughtering, towering head and shoulders as he did above most men.

The prisoners were dragged to the gibbet and for the most part the hangman excelled himself, delivering the half-alive bodies to the butcher for gutting and quartering whilst they still jerked and twisted. Harry Weaver closed his eyes. Lord, they had screamed like stuck pigs with the crowd roaring for more.

Fawkes was the last to be pushed up the hangman's ladder and Harry Weaver fixed the poor tortured body with his eye, willing courage into it with all his strength.

There was no movement as the hangman cut the rope and the lifeless body fell to the cobbles below. God had been good and the hangman too zealous. Fawkes was dead before his inert body received the slash of the butcher's cleaver . . .

A man stood beside Harry Weaver; a small, sparse man whose thin hair grew forward into a peak on his forehead, whose hooded eyes were dark and wary. He had lifted his hand above the heads of the crowd as each pathetic body was manhandled from the scaffold and traced the evil air with the sign of the Cross, giving a silent benediction.

It had been a risky thing to do, for the man was obviously a Jesuit. But no one seemed to have noticed, or if they did they had not cared and Harry Weaver murmured *Amen* each time the hand signed the cross of absolution.

Now it was over, the crowds gone. The sugared-apple sellers had counted their silver and the meat-pie men were away to the nearest tavern to empty their bulging pockets.

Harry Weaver hugged his cloak around him, clasping it tightly to stop the violent trembling of his limbs.

He was glad he had seen the killings, for now he had found a bitterness inside him he had never thought to possess and he would keep it smouldering there. He would pile his resentment and disgust upon the fire of his loathing and tomorrow, when he was ushered into the presence of Robert Cecil, that fire would leap into a fierce flame of hatred. Tomorrow he too would show Cecil the grit and granite that men of York were made of!

The summons to London had not been unexpected—he had known Cecil would send for him again and was a little glad, truth known, when after Christmas the letter from London was delivered.

Cecil's mark was on him, thought Harry bitterly, and now the misshapen devil was about to make play for his own.

He thinks I will work for him; do his spying and report on the movements of my neighbours. He imagines he has the power to buy me, that in return for his silence I shall be his to command.

He could almost hear the whispered, *"It is sad, Sir Harry, that you should be a bastard and the bastard at that of a known traitor. You are lucky to have kept your begetting quiet for so long. God in heaven—that red hair . . . !"*

But Harry Weaver was prepared for all that now. He knew and he didn't care! It only mattered that he should be his own man and true to himself and the two most wonderful people who had reared him as their own.

So he would stand there until Cecil had raked over the muck of years, then laugh in his evil little face.

"Aye, good my lord, I know it. I was fathered by Christopher Wakeman who lies dead beside Meg my mother at the crossing of the roads above Aldbridge. So shout it all over London; tell it to all the North Riding; stand on the topmost turret of Micklegate Bar and proclaim it to the whole of York county if you dare!

"But before you do it, think of the night of the twenty-sixth of October and the priory at Hoxton. Think of the page-boy and Thomas Ward and the letter that was hurried back to London. Do not seek to deny it, for I followed Mounteagle and the letter came straight back to its writer—to *you*, my lord of Salisbury!

"Remember all that before you seek to buy my services, and that I too have a tongue and can bawl louder than you!"

He straightened his shoulders and threw back his head, laughing defiance into the stinking London night.

Aye, tomorrow he'd toss back the Judas money and hoist Cecil with his own petard. Then he'd be on his way home again, free as the wind and his own man—for ever his own man . . .